the

CONSTANT
EYE

D0101283

BY THE SAME AUTHOR
The Last Look

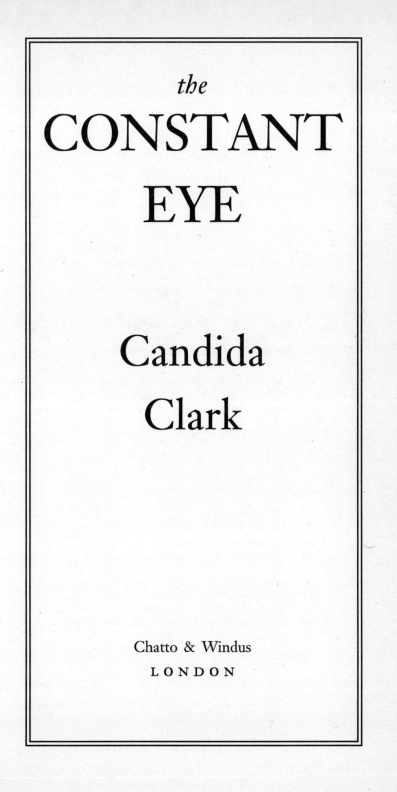

the
CONSTANT
EYE

Candida
Clark

Chatto & Windus
LONDON

Published by Chatto & Windus 2000

2 4 6 8 10 9 7 5 3 1

Copyright © Candida Clark 2000

Candida Clark has asserted her right under the
Copyright, Designs and Patents Act 1988 to
be identified as the author of this work

First published in Great Britain in 2000 by
Chatto & Windus
Random House, 20 Vauxhall Bridge Road,
London SW1V 2SA

Random House Australia (Pty) Limited
20 Alfred Street, Milsons Point, Sydney,
New South Wales 2061, Australia

Random House New Zealand Limited
18 Poland Road, Glenfield,
Auckland 10, New Zealand

Random House (Pty) Limited
Endulini, 5A Jubilee Road, Parktown, 2193, South Africa

The Random House Group Limited Reg. No. 954009
www.randomhouse.co.uk

A CIP catalogue record for this book
is available from the British Library

ISBN 0 7011 6909 5

Papers used by Random House are natural,
recyclable products made from wood grown in sustainable forests.
The manufacturing processes conform to the environmental
regulations of the country of origin

Typeset by Deltatype Ltd, Birkenhead, Merseyside
Printed and bound in Great Britain by
Mackays of Chatham plc

For Tim.

With many thanks to Rebecca Carter and Jonny Geller.

He went like one that hath been stunned,
And is of sense forlorn:
A sadder and a wiser man,
He rose the morrow morn.

From 'The Ancient Mariner' by Samuel Taylor Coleridge

One

I

She is sitting opposite me with her back to the direction the train is going. She smiles briefly, though not at me. I smile at her. 'This is pleasant, isn't this pleasant?' I say to her, flagging down a stewardess to order us some drinks. She perks up no end at this suggestion and I notice how transformed she is when she gets animated and focused on something, even if it is just ordering a drink.

Now the train is slipping out of the station real quiet, so I barely notice we're leaving, which also has something to do with the fact that I have my eye on her. I'm watching what she does, trying to work her out, thinking I have, to just the right degree mind you, not too much but still enough to keep me interested, enough to make me want to prove my suspicions right, which is how I like it and how it has always been with me.

See, I travel on trains a lot. If it's at all possible to take a train, rather than fly, then I do. I make it part of my trip, not just the means of getting there. And I love stations almost as much as I love trains. They are among the few places it's considered acceptable to move on from. Of course, that's the big idea with them. I can be free in a station, like nowhere else. No one wants to cling to me there or keep me put. More than anything, I hate to be tied down. It kills my soul and makes me afraid to my guts. If I'm honest, that's the main reason: the fear.

And trains, well they just give me hope that the fear will end. Trains are like the arteries and veins of a body, the network spreading, pumping across the land like life-blood, miraculous and fertile, endless with possibility.

I remember very clearly the first time I travelled by train. I was four. The journey was from London where my father was posted at that time, to a tiny village up in the north, on the coast. The tracks don't run that far any more, they stop at the town ten miles away, but back then they did. You had to change trains three times. It was a family holiday. We'd taken a house on the beach. The journey along the coastline was the best part of it: the sea sparkled like a dream and I jumped up and down the whole time, overwhelmed, as though it were magic. That feeling has stayed with me all my life. I even had my first fuck on a train, but that's another story.

The drinks arrive and we chink glasses, smirking at one another, and I give her my best smile, suave as hell and warm, too, as though to say: *you know that I know you're very beautiful, don't you?* which always works, in my experience. Trains are perfect for this kind of liaison. And if it doesn't work out, there's an in-built ending. No mess. No fuss or nuisance. Just a clean break at the final destination. *It was great to meet you, I have your number, in case I'm ever in town.* That kind of thing. It never fails. They always know this is how it will end, too, so they don't go getting funny ideas like they do in normal circumstances. Normal? I don't know. But I'm jumping the gun and I know it. All things considered, there's a good chance this one won't play ball. I haven't worked out whether that misty-eyed smile she's giving me is because she knows the score, or for some other reason. I feel curious to find out. Anyway, if it gets too complicated, I can always lose her in Paris when I change stations. I reckon that much is understood.

All of this passes in an instant. The wheels have barely finished their first rotation, is how it seems, and I've fixed her with an interested look so there's no mistaking what I'm aiming at. She can change seats or just ignore me if she likes, I mean, if she doesn't want to stay around to see what happens, what might happen between us. She might be chicken, she might not have the balls for it. She might be too uptight.

Some of them are. I've met them. They look at you like they're hot for it, they sit there crossing and uncrossing their legs like they can't sit still with the expectation, and then when it comes to it, when it comes to the moment they're supposed to follow you out the room or across the street into the darkness, or round the back of the bar or wherever it is, they giggle like virgins and totter away as fast as their misleading little heels will take them. It bores me to tears, I can tell you. And I still haven't quite decided which kind she is, which is nice. I like it like this, the uncertainty, and as I said, if it doesn't work out by Paris I can always get rid of her. *So*, I say to myself, *what have I got to lose?*

We're picking up speed now, skimming the tracks, cutting through the slate roof-tops and on past the dismal rows of tiny terraced houses which always puzzle me: how can anyone live there? Sometimes, but not now, I wish I was one of them, or at least someone capable of such a thing, living in a narrow house on the edge of nowhere. That kind of comfortable oblivion must have its advantages I guess, else why would so many people do it? But I already know the answer to this. And I realise it's just not something I could do myself. It would be like putting sticking plasters on my eyes so's I couldn't see, deliberately, knowing that to take them off would hurt like hell.

Outside, the day is glassy clear, so I can tell there's going to be frost tonight. The air itself looks still and there are no clouds whatsoever, just the endless grey, incredible, like there's been a mistake and the colour hasn't woken up yet, like the whole country's in mourning.

It is on days like this that I'm glad I'm a foreigner. Even though I have lived here most of my life, I still regard myself as a foreigner. It's like that with Americans. We can be citizens of nowhere and everywhere. Free to love wherever we chose to live without the burden of nostalgia or hate. I have languages and dark hair, dark eyes, too, so I can blend. Blend and watch. Make mental notes. Suck the situation dry and move on. Does that sound bad? It's not so bad really. It's how I like to live. And I give things back, too. I'm a good listener which is something people appreciate more than you might at first think. Someone with a spare ear and all the time in the world to listen.

I like to cajole. 'You can tell me. I don't want anything in return. I'll just listen. You can talk to me. I won't bite. Just keep talking.' These are the things I like to say. You'd be amazed how well people respond to this. It's like an avalanche. An abundant, flooding harvest. Words just pour out. One long vomit of pent-up disappointments. All I have to do is scoop them up and leave them to settle for a while until they're nice and ripe and then, hey presto, all the stories I could ever need. The mind is a magical thing that way. It fools you so sweetly.

You might think that something forgotten is also gone, but it just isn't so. Everything that happens to you, or everything you ever hear, is all lying in wait, simmering away right at the very back of your mind where no one else can get at it, take it away from you or even see it, which is the main point: the secrecy. And for a writer, secrecy equals a kind of freedom that's invaluable.

My theory is that being a writer is a bit like being a pirate. A dirty thief living outside the law, who, from time to time, forgets where his illicit treasure is stashed. So you live your life in a state of perpetual guilt, anguish and surprise. But it's the piratical stash, the stuff that goes on in the secret back-room of your mind that is the most precious, the stuff that counts. It's the better part of yourself – or maybe the worst. Certainly, it's all you've got and all you'll be left with in the end. See, I've got it sussed. Or perhaps I've just been lucky. Because it was very early on in life when I figured all this out and there's never been anything happen since then to prove me wrong.

All of this passes swiftly through my mind while I sit there opposite her. I take a quick look out the window as the distance slows down and everything close by speeds up and blurs. I love it when this happens. It clarifies all my suspicions about the different layers there are to time, even when you're not watching it, keeping your eye peeled, even then, it's layered, fast and slow, depending. So there's always going to be the layers of what you notice and what you are blind to or blinded by, everything falling through the sunny rays of your bright little eye, filtering things out according to it's own particular plan. I mean, according to what the watchful boys in the backroom of your mind see fit to let in. And there's always going to be stuff they don't let in and stuff they do, purely for reasons anonymous – at least, without a name you can put a sense to.

I turn to her, saying, 'We're really moving now aren't we?' Or some such remark but she's absorbed in her thoughts, staring out the window pretty much as I do myself when I'm travelling alone, which is less often than I'd like, since I find it almost impossible to resist the temptation of paying all my attention to whoever most interests me. And there's always someone. This time it's her, is all. But I'm glad that she's looking out of the window. It gives me chance to take a proper squint at her.

She's approaching thirty but has great bones, which in fact makes it difficult to tell her age. Fragile-seeming bones though, too. Clearly defined beneath her skin. A delicate nose. Very straight. A classically beautiful nose, I guess is how people might like to describe it. Large eyes, pale eyes, a kind of golden colour. They move around restlessly, not focusing on anything until suddenly, wham, they've got you fixed like a laser-beam, boring right into you like she knows exactly what you're thinking. Not disconcerting though, which is strange. There's something frank and honest, weirdly honest about her eyes. But they reveal nothing. They give nothing away, as though she has no conscious sense of her own history that she could even begin to retell to someone. Those eyes of hers could almost be empty, which intrigues me. It's as though she's managed to erase all immediate sensation from them. I say immediate sensation, because there's something way back behind their golden surface which I can't pin down yet.

She's a sensual woman, that's the main thing, so it could be that. That erased look of hers could be some kind of wild, flotsam abandonment to the here-and-now, careless of the piercing facts that might drag her down into her past. Her lips are really something. She has a wide, almost swollen-seeming mouth that shivers slightly the whole time as though she's thinking something she reckons she shouldn't be. I love that in a woman. That secrecy. It strikes me as honest. Everyone should have stuff inside them that ought to stay there. Stuff they just wish they could get out but know they can't, shouldn't, ought not to, really, not just yet. But they always will. In the end, they'll always let it out. It's just a question of time and getting the circumstance right. I have good feelings about her. Just look at her! Those lips!

It's her hair that troubles me the most. It's like she's growing out a razor-short cut but this doesn't at all fit with the way she's dressed. She's got on a silky-looking dress. Black, with a tiny flowery pattern on it in pinks and greens and a low v-neck to it so I can see the slightest swelling of her breasts when she leans sideways, like now. Over this she has a little yellow cardigan made of something soft like cashmere. It looks like she's wearing stockings, too, pale flesh-coloured, nice and smooth over her slim calves and tiny little ankles. Hell, they look fragile. I can't help but notice how tiny they are, about the same size as my wrists. Her feet are strapped lightly into a pair of black high-heeled shoes that it's difficult to see how they're fit to walk in. They're not that high but they're delicate. Not much more than a few straps fastened together. I love it when you can tell a woman likes shoes, that she likes her feet as well, at least enough to want to make them prettier than they already are.

I must've been looking rather too hard at her feet because when I look up at her face again, she's staring at me with a puzzled expression, a bit worried, too, like I might get down on the floor and try to eat those little feet of hers, which, to tell the truth, I wouldn't mind doing, they look so nice and sweet.

So I give her a big easy smile to reassure her. She smiles back and takes a deep glug of her whisky as though she's nervous, almost, but preoccupied with something else.

'Tell me,' I say, 'are you going to see your family for Christmas?' She shoots me an odd look when I ask her this perfectly ordinary question. It's 23 December, after all. Not like it's the middle of summer or something crazy, which makes me wonder what's in her head. I want to find out now though, that's the trouble. I've got the scent. I know I want to see it through. Perhaps it was just those feet and those damn lips that did it, but I confess, I'm hooked. 'Or is it your husband, I mean does your husband live in France?' I say to test her. 'Yes, that's it,' she says, fixing me with a stare that I can't make out at all, until she looks away suddenly as though that's the end of our conversation and I don't get more of an answer than that, at least not just yet.

And then a moment descends upon us which I recognise only too well. I can almost hear her brain-processes whirring away as she assesses the situation. Should she take out a book? she's thinking, or should she face the music, weather the storm with me, face the fact that sooner or later I'm going to pose the question: will she or won't she? Either verbally I'm going to ask her, or merely by touching her hand or her ankle, or perhaps even her hair. Accidentally, of course. Or so it would seem. Just the merest touch. Just to let her know, so there can be no mistaking it when I get up and walk away down the corridor to the loo. Or even draw it out, some like it better that way, and wait until Paris, suggest dinner or somewhere quiet we could go, and then watch her little pseudo-surprised smile. It's always like that, a little edgy twitching at the corner of their mouths to let me know they want it, that they're crazy for it, that they've got to have it or else they'll go insane, or some such.

But we haven't got to this stage yet. Easy does it, I'm thinking to myself, don't want to scare her off. She looks like she might be the frightened-off kind. So I pretend not to be paying her much attention, to let her make up her mind herself, without any pressure. I gawp out the window like she's been doing, watching the city thinning out into lower houses, more green, more trees and the spread of land widening, crouching way away over the rim of the earth, as though the whole island is held together like a drum skin nice and tight by the hidden towns and cities beyond the horizon, like it's been pegged down by the weight of the buildings and here we are in this lovely train, slicing a metal knife slice through it, not part of the place at all but a cut through it like a wound you've just got to accept, a dumb gash meaning nothing in itself but still troubling, like an anthill with the swarm hot for honey on top, creeping and itching through whoever might imagine it.

'So why do you like trains so much?' someone's saying and it's her. This shocks me momentarily, like she's been watching the unhinging of my mind for a moment and realised that that's all it comes down to: I like trains.

So I laugh my big easy laugh. 'Does it show that much?' I say, as if it were the most natural thing in the world for her to have worked this out when all I was doing was gawping out the window for a moment to give her the time to make up her mind whether she wanted it or not. *So I guess this means she does*, I'm thinking, saying to her in my mind, *I want to eat you, you know that don't you?* And she actually blushes. Maybe she is telepathic? I mean really telepathic. It's possible, isn't it? And I hope to God I'm not blushing too. But I suspect I am by the way she suddenly flashes me a brilliant smile which lights up her whole face so's her eyes dance and glint like hot coals with drips of petrol thrown on.

'You like them too? Trains?' I ask her, and she nods like a kid, a wild nod like she suspects the wrong words will come out if she tries to say anything, and I'm struck by the irrelevant energy to this gesture. It makes me wonder what she might be thinking. There's something child-like in her madly nodding head that worries me.

Then she says nothing. She just looks at me as though I'm the one who's supposed to be doing the talking, not her, and I realise it's going to be more difficult than I imagined, getting her to open up and pour her little heart out to me. 'So have you been through the tunnel before?' I ask, thinking I'll have to take it slow, but that's OK, it's a while yet to Paris, there's no rush.

'Oh yes, of course,' she says breezily, 'I'm used to it.' Her voice sounding suddenly different. Tighter, lower, even another accent. She looks different, too. Something falls away from her limbs and regathers itself like a sudden change of clothes. She settles herself back in her seat, her shoulders rearranged in a new curve that is sultry, languid, as she takes a sip of her drink, keeping her eyes on me this time, watching me over the rim of her glass, a predatory look, there's no mistaking it and I don't mind admitting this scares the hell out of me.

It's like looking in a mirror. As though she is mimicking precisely the look I just gave her a few minutes ago, the *I want to eat you* look and I'm not quite sure what I should do. So I turn to the window to escape those hot gold eyes for a second or two, taking a hefty swig from my whisky in the meantime, but not able to avoid seeing the way she is flexing her ankles. I can see her doing this in the reflection of the window, slowly turning her ankles round and round like a horny little cat on heat, arching its back and rubbing up against me, all trepidation gone now. And she's even making a kind of almost-groaning noise, like she's pretending to yawn or stretch but really just trying to let me know she's hot for it. It's like she's a different woman all of a sudden, as though there are no secrets between us and we're both fixed on the same thought, fair and square, no mystery and no messing: we both want it.

Can this be true? So soon? I haven't even given her the chance to spill her soul yet. This is too fast. *Is this too fast?* What the hell. I could like it like this and maybe I don't always have to do things the same way. Maybe I'll do it differently this time.

So I summon up the courage to take a look around at her and she's staring at me from beneath her eyelashes like a regular high-class whore with all the time in the world just so long as she gets what she's after in the end and just so long as the end is soon and it will be if she keeps looking at me like this. Because any second now I'll have to cart her off and fuck her pretty little brains out, is what I'm thinking. I'll have to do it.

'But first,' she says, 'tell me a bit about yourself why don't you?' And she's grinning, too, and I'm losing my wits with the idea that she's reading my goddamn mind. How else could she think to say 'but first'?

I'll but first you madam I'm thinking, and she's smiling at me still, a slim little smile edging across her face as she squirms around in her seat, pretending to get comfortable, her dress slipping further and further up her thighs so I catch a glimpse of stocking-top. *Say it ain't so!* I'm hard as a fucking rock as she crosses and re-crosses her legs, real nonchalant, stretching those damn ankles some more just so I have to take a look at them, almost because it would be rude not to, you know? So I do, and there's a question in her eyes, as though she's impatient for me to start telling her my life story. *And why the hell should she care?* is what I want to know. *Why the hell should she?*

'Tell me where you were born,' she's saying and I smile at her in a way that I suspect makes me look like a maniac with fangs, my jaw clenched like an idiot with the strain of not thinking about my goddamn cock.

'Born?' I say, wondering what the hell she's playing at, 'Brooklyn, New York.' And she nods as though she knew this already, and to encourage me, too, and I'm resisting the urge to say 'We know the score. Let's quit this pussyfooting around and get down to it.' But she's nodding at me slightly, waiting for me to go on and I'm thinking, *This is unreal. Why should I tell her anything? What right has she got to know? Why the hell's she trying to weigh me down with all these goddamn facts? What's she getting at?*

'You should read my books, really, if you want to know about me. It's all in there,' I say, trying to sound jovial, hoping to shut her up.

'That's unfair,' she says. 'That's cheating, you know it is.' It's true, I do know it is. But what the hell else am I supposed to say? 'So you're a writer, I know that much,' she says, now the coquette, clutching at her lover's shirt with red nails, as if to lay her claim *See, I have this on you.*

I fist my hands together on the table between us, giving her an *If you must know* look, sighing deeply, too, so she gets the message, deciding that I might as well go ahead and tell her the lousy facts, the story she's so hungry for. 'Well, we left America when I was very young. Four, in fact,' I say to her. 'My father was in the diplomatic corps and he got posted to London so we went there. I still feel a connection to Brooklyn though, something that goes right back. Visions of our house, the red-brown bricks, the dark rooms with huge ceilings I couldn't see the end of, ceilings that just went on and on, I remember that. And the heat, all summer, I remember the heat, which is strange don't you think? Just vague sensations but powerful. So whenever it's hot, or if I look up at the ceiling in the room of a tall house, I get that whipsnap realisation that these were the first things I ever felt about the world. It's nice. Makes me feel like I've got a bona fide past which is difficult sometimes to square with writing, if you see what I mean. You're too often in the business of remaking your past, not consolidating it at all, but knocking it all down and saying it happened a different way.'

I peek a look at her because I suddenly realise I've rattled on in one breath and it probably makes no sense, because I'm that unused to talking about myself, is the truth. It's something I never do, as a rule. In fact, I avoid it at all costs, unless it's a straightforward lie I'm spinning. I prefer to listen, to eke things out of other people, hear their stories, like I said. So I look at her to see how she's taking it, whether she really wanted to hear any of this, or was just being polite, or trying to cool me off, play with me, or I don't know what. But she's concentrating hard, understanding exactly what I'm saying.

She wants to hear more, too. I can tell from her little wrinkled eyebrows which are all bowed up real sweet as though she's doing maths. I hadn't noticed how sweet her eyebrows are until now, which makes me grin and she grins back, just to return the favour. 'Go on,' she says. 'This is only the beginning.' And I don't even stop to consider this remark which makes the hair on my balls crackle with expectation. I merely carry on telling her about myself, just like she wants me to.

II

Beyond the windows, the fields are zipping past fast faster and the sun is coming out, though only a little bit at a time, as though reluctant as I am to give away too much all at once. Over beyond the first line of flying trees there's a dirty lake with a lustre like platinum, cool in the greasy sunlight while we slip by, getting to know one another better. But that's a lie. It's me that's doing all the talking. So while part of me is saying *This is nice, isn't this nice?* the other part isn't so sure at all. Because like I said, I'm so unused to giving anything away about myself. Especially on trains. I think of trains as the places where I give away the very least of all.

'So I was four when we came to England and soon enough all my brownstone memories were disappearing, being replaced by the smells of the house we moved into. A great big town house in a square, really grand, great big ceilings, too, but this time airy and full of light. No more sap-coloured corners like before. No nicotine corridors either. The whole thing unbelievably refined and elegant. I felt lucky. I didn't take it for granted. Not the shiny black piano, the huge garden, the whole top floor for me to play in, none of it, especially when my mother died – I was around seven at this time. The most beautiful woman. Long pale hair, Chinese-straight but silver-coloured, blonde like a clean labrador, we had one of those back then, too, all part of the new image my father had to fit into, wanted to fit us into. Cancer. Not seven when she died but seven when I found out she'd got it. So the next two years were waiting, which put a great strain on my father, though you wouldn't have been able to tell if you hadn't known his movements intimately.

'He travelled slightly less often. She went to fewer parties. But when she actually died he was ruined. Everything was finished. The house, the breezy tall windows, picnics, the smell of silk and magnolia blossoms my mother used to wear – it filled the house. Everything went. She was his life. I hadn't realised it until then. The cliché. You never do realise. I'd imagined his work was for himself but it wasn't. It was all for her. I was sent to school and my father went back to America and that was that. I saw him in the vacations only. He died when I was in my last year before going up to university. After that I lived with his sister in Connecticut. She tried to mother me but saw there was no point. I hated school. You're supposed to in England aren't you? Then university. Great few years. Completely useless. I spent the whole time writing and working on my drink habit. Published my first book the year after I went down and the rest you can read at Hatchards.'

Her eyes surprised me. I'd been watching the speeding cows and the wrecked progression of fences and hedgerows and hadn't noticed her expression. I'd expected, I'd almost hoped for intrigued boredom. *Enough, I was only being polite.* I'd expected her eyes would say that but there was something else instead: disbelief.

'So how was it really? It all stops there?' she says, with an odd gulp of laughter. 'This is the kind of thing you're going to fob me off with?' Then she reaches across the table towards me and takes a hold of my wrists in her hands, which are little but hell they're strong, and she's almost hurting me for God's sake. How's such a thing possible? 'You've told me nothing, you shithead,' she says affectionately, still holding my wrists but looser now and rubbing her thumbs along the insides where it's soft. Then she drops one hand absentmindedly so it clunks to the table top as she starts looking out of the window, the seductress all gone and something unbearably sorrowful and hangdog come over her face, her shoulders drooping, too. It's as though she has gone back to being the child she was earlier, but not quite, and I wonder where all these different people are coming from.

I have to shake her hand slightly then, to remind her I'm here, and when I do this she turns to me and blushes, pulling her arms right away, as though it was me who took hold of her. Her eyes register me as if for the first time, as though she's never before clamped eyes on me and isn't sure just yet that she likes what she sees. I sit back hard in my seat, not knowing what to do. It spooks me, that look she's giving me. It really spooks me and I'm glad when the other look, the seductress, comes back, though it seems less resolute this time.

'So are you going to let me get to know you, or are you the type just to spin any old line? Which type are you?' she says, twirling a little piece of hair around between her fingers, looking at me from beneath her eyelashes again like nothing has happened.

I laugh. I expect it was a nervous laugh, because I certainly am nervous and we've only just left London and, as you can imagine, my thoughts are turning to either getting away from her right now, or dragging her off somewhere we can sort this one out in privacy. Doing something, at least.

This is when I feel her stockinged toe somehow worming its way into the sliver of bare skin between my sock and trouser leg. She's turned away from me and seems intent on staring at the scenery, so much so that I could almost imagine it was someone else's touch. *So it's a game is it?* I'm thinking, feeling her agile toes rub up against my leg like a curious little animal. I lift my own foot up to see if I can get any kind of an angle on her legs, but it doesn't work with my goddamn clumpy shoes on. She's wearing a secretive smile now so I think she's worked out this fact and finds it really too amusing for words.

Then all of a sudden she turns around to face me, saying simply, 'Come on,' getting up breezy as anything and strolling off towards the loo without looking back. I'm stunned, I can tell you, shocked rigid and hard as hell with the cheek of it. What a girl! And I'm up in a flash, following her swaying skirt off down the corridor and into the loo.

She's standing in there turned away from me, facing the outside wall of the train where the window usually is. Her back is tiny and motionless. I notice the way the thin shiny fabric of her dress stretches across the curve of her waist, outlining the faint ridges along her spine. She's standing dead still as though she's watching something. 'What can you see?' I say to her, real quiet, pulling the door closed behind me, and she jumps round, squirming like a scorpion against the wall, looking as though she's afraid she'll lash out at me, won't be able to help herself.

'Come here,' I say, 'I'm not going to eat you. You're a dark horse,' I tell her as I pull her towards me, folding her up in my arms, suddenly feeling fraternal more than anything else, though hot for her, too, but wondering, really wondering what she's up to, expecting this is all part of an elaborate ploy. Some of them are like that, putting on an act so that they don't have to take any responsibility for what they get up to. It's usually the wildest ones who do this. They just can't seem to square their sweating clawing screaming panting antics with the sweet girl they like to think they are when they walk down the street, or sit sipping tea with their mothers, or whoever it is. It's a good disguise, I suppose, so I don't begrudge them it. Anyway, I know all about disguises, who am I to talk?

So here she is all wrapped up in my arms and I'm busy trying to fathom her out, when I feel her wet cat's tongue lapping a neat pattern against the side of my neck, and her hands pressed either side of my backbone so that her hips grind against the tops of my thighs and I can feel her shape fit snugly against me, her belly no doubt finding out the shape of me, too, since the moment she stands like this my cock springs to attention, and it's a pact: two bodies pressed together sealing something or other unspoken. The hot flesh wanting without needing a single word. The language one of wet skin and tangling breath, that makes no sense other than this perfect articulation of need, whilst outside, somewhere far away from us, the cool train keeps a rhythm for us to return to, though many minutes from now because right now she's biting the shell of my skin, cracking me like I was a tired old nut, easily, between her sharp teeth. Dangerous teeth. The kind to give you nightmares, really. Precise enough not to worry me at this moment but later I know I'll dream of teeth and think of her.

But now she's got her right knee wedged up against the sink, her left arm pushing herself upwards against my shoulder so I'm ground back against the door. *Did we lock the door?* I wonder, to keep myself slowed down, since if I don't edge some brink of anxiety into my mind this very second then it'll all be over, and then what?

She levers herself up so that our hips meet, then her hips get higher and her left leg slips itself around my waist, clinging to me while we kiss. Her lips are honeyed, just made for being bitten, and those sharp little teeth, as I'd suspected, nibbling a dangerous track across my throat, the whole set-up really perfect: her weight and fragile ankles, wide mouth and the way her arse cheeks fit nicely into my hands so's I can lift her easily and hold her still for a moment while I release my poor damn cock from its torment, trapped against the rough inside of my jeans, before lowering her down in one easy slide on to the smooth wet slip of my cock, her cunt.

So she's shuddering now slightly while I hold her there, bracing myself with my left hand against the back of the door as the train judders momentarily and she lets out a tiny yelping noise, stretching backwards so she can grind herself harder down on to me and I can feel her wet cuntlips tight around me as I get myself wedged into position, taking hold of her arse cheeks again, one in each hand, so I can lift and lower her, nice and slow, not so slow, lifting and lowering her, feeling the warm slide of cuntcock getting a rhythm that's all our own, right now, for this moment. I realise I've got my eyes shut, so I open them, not remembering the last time I shut my eyes when I fucked someone – it was a long time ago – and she's got her wide eyes fixed on my face like she's never seen me before. This should alarm me, I guess, but now I'm imperturbable, concentrating on the lifting lowering wet cuntcock rhythm we've got going. So our eyes are boring into one another's and she's clinging for dear life around my neck, her right foot braced against the sink for leverage, her left leg around my waist for support, the whole thing perfectly worked out so that we fit, with no rough bits, like a well oiled fuckmachine, bouncing along with the rattling tracks slipping past beneath us, the speeding bite of the click clack tracks oozing along so fast we're the only things slow, but speeding up now, her eyes boring into mine and mine boring into hers like the four eyeballs are stuck on two parallel wires.

I'm wondering when she's going to look away like women do. Helpless at the last moment. Screwing their eyes up so I can't get a look into the filthy dark pits of their neediness, which is what I most want to do, since it's then they know they're out of control and they've just got to face it, just got to accept it. I could pull out at any minute and my cock rhythm would go on without them, but they need this slip and lifting lowering however much they might play and pretend they don't. In a way I pity them for needing it and thank God I was born a man, thank God, so I can admire from a distance that certainly *is* pity not admiration, though I like to say it amounts to the same thing. But who the fuck do I care about convincing anyway? Eyes trammelled into one burning stream and any minute now she'll close her eyes. Any minute now I won't get to see the dark pit of her grim lust. Any minute.

But her arms are going from around my neck and she places her hands either side of my face, covering my ears so I can't hear the train. Hardly hear anything. Just see her open-wide eyes melting like boiling gold. Two unembered lumps of too-hot stuff refusing to close. I can feel the quaking hard shudder start up inside her like her guts are on fire and groaning with the lovely pain of it, grunting shittishly like pig organs, obscenely pleasurable, deep inside her, and she's smiling like a buddha serene as sweet peas at dawn, delicate pale despite the hot bubbling I can feel in her loins, her guts filling her up with bliss which is triumph, too, as she feels the end of my cock exploding inside her so that I stagger, my legs buckling with the weight of her, screwing my eyes up tight hard so she can't see me flicker, guttering going out dead in my eyes at that moment when I give up the fight, returned too fast to the juddering lift and lower of the train tracks' hot click past and beneath us, the hot click past, and beneath us, going on and on, despite the abrupt caesura of exploding staggering, before, finally, I can open my eyes again as I steady myself, leaning back hard against the door.

She's looking at her face in the mirror. Her hands flutter across her downy hair and she wipes away an imaginary something from her left cheekbone. On the floor is a pair of cream lace knickers which I suppose are hers. She picks them up and instead of putting them back on, she folds them over twice and puts them into her pocket. I realise that she must have whipped them off in the second before I followed her into the loo and it puzzles me – the thought of her taking them off in one swift action before turning her back to the door and calmly facing the wall where the window should be.

She runs her hands over her dress, smoothing down the already smooth fabric. An involuntary, copied gesture that I recognise from thousands of other women and I know that that is the only reason why she does it. I almost expect her to say *Well?* when she turns back to me, because her face has an air of mild amusement about it. But instead she leans towards me and puts a hand on to my shoulder, cupping it there for a moment, as if considering something for the first time.

I look down at myself, my jeans around my ankles and my limp cock dangling in time to the train and and I feel wildly inappropriate all of a sudden with her hand on my shoulder like an aunt. So I pull up my trousers real quick, trying not to catch her eye, because she's watching me intently like she's waiting for clues. I'm determined not to give her anything to go on, why the hell should I? Jesus! Then the train starts slowing up slightly, there's the sound of grinding brakes and the tightening scent of burning and it must be the station we're at, so I hitch up my belt buckle and she follows me out of the loo, back into the corridor. I go off the other way, saying 'I'll just be a minute,' needing to walk around a bit. Thinking *I should get the hell out of here*, checking she's going back to her seat, watching her back walk away, swaying slightly as the train comes to a stop at the only station before the tunnel and before Paris.

I go to stand by one of the doors in the corridor, leaning back against the wall, catching my breath. Outside the window, the platform is empty apart from a little family on the other side.

Parents and two small children. I think of my own almost-children for a moment, but only a moment because what's a guy to do tormenting himself with thoughts like that.

It's steely grey outside now, the colour of a heat haze but cold, and the trees' motionless fingers scratch the thin mirror of sky like a punishment. I have a sore neck where she bit me and around my waist there's the echo of her weight signalling the start of a bruise. Motionless, I can see more clearly the leaping bones crush against themselves. In my mind's eye, I can better remember the shape of our breathing as we fought to find the place where we could finish off our idiot, beastish needs. And even now I'm thinking about her sitting there with her wet cunt soaking into the slippery surface of her dress, reminding her of what she is, and I'm getting hard again just thinking about it.

But I'm sure as hell not going to do anything about it just yet, though I'm baffled by the fact that I'm wanting her so soon, because it isn't usually the way with me. Fucking usually cures me of women. At least, it cures me of whichever woman in particular it is at the time.

The doors to the rest of the corridor suck closed and I'm in a little silent box of thinking while the train stays still. Beyond the window, the family walk away out of sight down to the far end of the platform, so there's no sign of anyone whatsoever, no living thing apart from me and the birds hidden away somewhere I can't see them. It's just me, the train, the empty station and that's it, apart from the bruises around my waist and the teeth-prints on my neck.

I stop breathing for a moment so that I can hear the soundless space dead still around me, as though motion has been boxed up so I can get a proper look at it, and here it is, and I can't see any sense to it, though I thought I would have. The fact of the silent un-motion, the empty station, me in the train, I'd thought these things would add up to something, but it's just that and no more, the station seeming like a wart or fungus growing parasitical upon the cool bleeding vein of metal track. For the first time, it seems plausible that one day I'll be careless about trains, disinterested, and the thing I've lived by will be lost and I won't even notice, still less care. But now this is just a glimmer, only the edge of a thought and it leaves me unmoved, thank God.

So when the train engine starts farting back into life as we slip out of the station and I haven't jumped off, strolled away down the platform as I'd intended, or at least hoped I would, with the family waving stupidly at the train flying past full of strangers, the children's little paws grasping hopelessly at the empty air, faces red-cheeked and confident in the icy stillness, when all this goes on, it's the easiest thing in the world and not at all difficult as I'd begun to fear, to straighten myself up and stroll back down the corridor.

I stop a stewardess on the way to order more drinks, thinking it would be grand to smoke a cigar, even though I haven't had one for months, making a secret decision to go to that tobacconist I like, in the Marais, to get some of those lovely *Romeo y Julietas* I used to smoke, take the girl there, too. Then maybe afterwards to a restaurant I know nearby with dark corners and sympathetic waiters who know when to leave you alone and when not to notice that you've left the restaurant together for a few minutes. But here I am jumping the gun again.

All these thoughts go skimming through my mind as I stroll back down the rows of seats, looking for her. She doesn't seem to be there yet and in fact I just passed by the place we were sitting. So I backtrack, checking the seat numbers, and feel a sudden rush of relief because her bag is still where she left it and I realise that I almost expected her to have run off, just like I'd intended to myself. But there's her bag, so she probably just went off to the loo to fix her make-up.

I sit down and get comfortable. The stewardess brings the drinks and I say, 'She'll be back in a minute,' about the empty space, feeling stupid to have said that, because the stewardess shoots me a look, as though the thought that she *wouldn't* be back never entered her head. I mean, why would anyone question such a thing? But it makes me uneasy and I wonder if I'm getting old, the fact that I care that things went so fast between us. *Why should it bother me?* I'm wondering. I've got what I really wanted and sooner than I'd hoped to get it, so what's the problem? But the minutes tick by. I'm looking at them ticking by on my watch, wondering what she's up to, despising myself for getting so anxious.

III

I guess you could describe me as a happy man. But I hate to wait. I just hate it. Women are made to wait all the time – for men, babies, the passage of inevitable pain. It's part of the reason they're usually so downtrodden.

And what am I doing now? Waiting. I'm waiting for her to come back. Waiting to see how things will turn out. So I swallow a mouthful of whisky and pick up the paper, not focusing on the jumping words, trying to pretend I'm doing something other than wait.

The day speeds past outside the window. I can see cows and pigs stuck to the green flooding backdrop, low-lying farmhouses with their motionless curls of coal smoke forever twisted up against the sky, and scooped-out black earth misplaced beside the gutted hillsides as the train slices up the minutes with a thundering slash of metal and engine stench.

I remember a hotel I stayed in once where a ninety-year-old woman had just died. She'd lived there since she was twenty. She had run away from her family to meet up with her lover. They were to be married in secret. But he didn't turn up. She wrote him every day, so the story went, telling him she was there and waiting for him. He never replied, never arrived, so she merely lived there, waiting, until she died. It needn't be true because it is true anyway about most women. It's how they live. Always on the brink. Always forgiving. Always waiting. Bovine and expectant. I hate that. It fills me with disgust.

I flick the edges of my paper to straighten it out, considering this story and wondering how long I'd wait for someone. Minutes? Hours? Years? Someone passes me in the aisle and I pretend to look away, thinking for a moment that it's her, hoping it's her. But the woman passes by and it's someone else and I realise that I've been holding my breath, a quick in-breath of expectation. *For God's sake what's up with me?*

So I get back to looking at the newspaper, trying not to notice the way that when I sit with my back pressed against the seat I can feel the slight tenderness where the bruise is forming around waist height, which makes me smile, feeling suddenly roguish. *And what the hell does it matter if she doesn't come back? Who gives a damn? I've got what I wanted, haven't I? I only wanted to fuck her, after all,* I tell myself, lying, wishing I'd managed to play it differently, eke her story out of her, just prise that lid off for a moment so's I could take a look before moving on.

But like I said, I'm a happy man. Genuinely happy. It takes more than this to unsettle me. It's just that I'm unused to being made to wait. I've arranged everything so that I don't have to wait for anything if I don't want to. It's rare that I encounter any nuisance. Besides, I don't stand for it. I don't need to. I've made something of my life. It's a success. So why worry? I figure I have nothing to worry about. Apart from the big things, naturally, the things I make it my business to worry about.

By that I mean that writing itself is a form of worrying, at least in my opinion. But it's not *lying down to die worrying* and the difference is everything. It's where I deal with my worries, not where I pretend I don't have them and sure as hell not where I give in to them. See, I don't exist anywhere but my books. I am nothing unless I can also find a way to say what I am. I feel nothing, unless I can write down something of what it's like. And what is reality if not a landscape of those things that are felt most nearly, a world you can't but believe in? That's the place I'm at when I write. Worrying and writing, as though my life depends on it. Say it's just fiction, but everything else exists only as lead-footed shadows of the real thing: those first bursts of creation, hot twitch at the edge of all beginnings.

You still need to ask why I do it? Because I'm shit-scared of death. Why else? But it's not a question of aiming for immortality. It's just a fixated longing for an other, lighter, truer life, while this fact-heavy one hangs about my neck, dragging me down towards death, packed full of lies. Yet every day is hard when you're trying to look for a solution you know can't be found. Trying to find a way out of something patently without ways out, but still trying, still kicking at the corners in agitation, attentive to every change in the prison even when there is no change. But like I said, I'm a happy man, so I don't let these things bother me on a practical basis. Ask anyone, they can see I've got it all worked out, plain as day. How else would I be able to go on? How would it be possible for anyone to go on? Just because these are words doesn't mean they offer any kind of protection now, does it?

But it's a lie when they tell you it's not possible to plan your life, guard against any eventuality. It's the easiest thing in the world to plan how things will turn out and then to stick to the plan like a fly to glue. Get in the soup and stay there! That's the easy part. The difficult bit is doing things differently once you've found the best way right at the start of the game. Then you spend the whole time measuring up the pieces till they fit and there's not a moment to spare for figuring out how to do things any other way. Travel by train and you'll see the truth of this statement soon enough, with everything moving along so sweetly and in adamant syncopation like a dead promise, unheard.

It is then that I hear her laughter. I hear it as if from another planet, somewhere beyond violence, the weight of frustration dogging my entire world with stinking, paddy little footsteps, prancing about to remind me, so I feel the sting of unfamiliarity like a whack to the jaw from an invisible hammer *What the hell's going on?*

I look at my watch and see she's only been gone around five minutes, yet already she's found someone she feels fit to laugh with, *What the hell*, deciding right then that I'll ignore the faithless bitch. *Who does she think she is, for God's sake. She imagines I'll wait for her, not be bothered by the fact that we've just fucked. We did fuck, didn't we fuck? And she's gone off with someone else so soon?*

So I sit there fuming, really livid and not sure why, or what to do about it, reminding myself that I'm a happy man and a successful one too, so why on earth should I go around thinking such things, now of all times? The worst part of it is: she's spoilt this train journey for me. I look out of the window, grimacing, watching my scowl in the reflection, pissed off and brooding, trying to decide what to do.

Then she's laughing again, the little tinkling laughter of a first class whore. But I've got to admit, she has a pretty laugh, the kind that suggests she really means it and I reflect that I haven't heard her laugh yet today and this pisses me off no end. *Why didn't I make her laugh?* I wonder. *What's wrong with me that she doesn't find any reason to laugh?* The stewardess goes past at this point and so I flag her down, 'Would you be so kind as to hot-foot it to the bar for another drink?' And this time she doesn't seem to expect me to order one for the girl which makes me mad. *Does she think I've been ditched? Why's she looking at the empty seat with that superior smile on her face? What is this?* So I order two drinks and fix the stewardess with a look, daring her to defy me.

Once she's gone, I wait until she's right out of sight, away down the aisles, then I lean across slightly to see if I can see the girl and there she is. At least, there's her ankle. She's doing that thing with it, arching and turning it around, dangling it there like an insult, and now she's stopped laughing and from the angle of her legs I can tell that she's leaning forwards towards whoever she's with to tell him some secret, no doubt. Even though she wouldn't tell me a single damn thing, already she's telling him something. And that's the worst part of it, the part I find difficult to square with my vision of her with those eyes boring into mine just a few minutes ago like they were on stalks with the goddamn pleasure of it all, not caring about another solitary thing apart from the lifting, lowering rhythm we got going on so easy it seemed almost natural that it happened as it did, the whole thing unfolding like a neat story all thought out beforehand, and then here she is laughing with someone else and so soon.

The day is darkening beyond the thick glass and I watch the trees begin to bend in the creeping wind from off the channel which will be soon, I reckon, not long now. Then it will be a different country and all of this can just slip away from me for all I care. England, her, the waving children, the friendless fields that mean nothing to me whatsoever, just like the fields on the other side of the sea, all of it really the domain of aliens, not people like me in any way.

I wonder if there will be a frost in Paris. I look at the trees here and like to imagine that I can tell there will, from the way there seems to be some kind of a tension around the tips of the branches, as though an electric current of freeze has been passed up through the land from many miles away, fingering its way up through the nervous, fleshy trunks, making the branch-tips rigid like fear. This is how it seems to me at any rate and I'd rather think of this than of her laughing with that man she's with, whoever the hell it is. And why should I care anyway, more to the point? She's a girl I fucked on a train and so what?

I get myself wedged into the side of my seat so that I can watch her legs turning and wriggling around while I decide what to do about it. She has very narrow insteps, I notice, with a high arch, flexible-looking, too, from the way she's bending and curling up her toes, her right foot almost completely out of her shoe by now, dangling that little slip of leather by the very last strap, waggling her foot around like she knows I'm watching. But what do I care? I just sit like this anyway, regardless of what she might be up to, though leaning across slightly so I can get a better look, feeling the seat-back's pressure against my spine where those very same toe-claws I'm watching right now lacerated my skin with a delicate puncture, back then when the thump thump of our sweet fucking became something not enough for me, was really more like a new beginning, so there I've said it. Because still she's told me nothing yet already is yakking on to that other person and that can't be right. I'm reminded, by the abrasive fabric's rub against my skin, of a time as a child, bare knees scuffed against harsh carpet as I crouched outside my parents' door late one night.

It was black in the house and the only light was the cut along the side of the door to their bedroom where I had my eye fixed, trying to see around the angle but not able to, so having to watch them in the mirror. I felt like I was at the movies and I thought I had a pretty good idea about what adults did together when they got to be alone. I reckoned I knew all about that.

My mother sat at her dressing table, brushing out her pale hair, endless strokes, obsessive strokes like marking time or filling time to stop it up, full up, so nothing else could get in there and happen in its place, just the hair-brushing and her eyes lighting their way to the mirror's reflection. My knees ached with crouching. The dog was running in its sleep downstairs and I could hear its tail thumping a haphazard beat alongside my mother's rhythmic brushing and I wondered if she could hear it too. My father left by the side door to go into the dressing room and I listened to the soft thwack of clothes-hanging as he undressed. She didn't stop brushing.

While he was gone, though, she touched the mirror, just once and tentatively too, almost like she'd seen a ghost, but like someone would in a play when the cliché takes away the shock, so it's more the memory of someone else's having seen a ghost and not your own memory at all – that's how she did it. She looked tired. Her skin had the appearance of simmering milk. There was something terrifyingly insubstantial about it. The paleness transfixed me. I almost expected her to peel it off.

Her fingers darted back from their little touch of the mirror, going straight to her lips like she'd just planted a kiss on someone's face that she shouldn't have done. I'd seen her do something similar a thousand times with me when she was afraid I'd be embarrassed by her kisses at school. What she didn't realise was how much I craved them, the scented swoosh of her pale hair across my face, as her lips, always trembling, touched me lightly on my cheek or the side of my head amongst my damp child's hair, her long-fingered hand finding a place to go behind my head to hold me there so she could give me that kiss. But there – her hand darted back to her lips and then fell down like a bird shot dead on to the dressing table where I could see its fingers' instinctive rigor mortis, tightly gripping the edge as though she was afraid she'd fall off.

Father came back in at this moment and her back went rigid as, with her other hand, she carried on brushing her hair, the hideous smoothness of her strokes like a punishment. He seemed to feel it, because I heard him saying, 'Come to bed, darling. You've brushed your hair long enough. Come on over here.'

She gets up at this point like a zombie and I am suddenly afraid for her, I don't know why, but the tone of his voice doesn't match the brushing of her hair and I want him to notice that she has been crying, but he doesn't seem to. She seems to forget it too, because she goes across to the bed, slipping off her robe, so underneath she's only got on a slip thing made of silk and lace the colour of her milky face, like death.

She gets into bed beside him and leans across to her light, flicking it off saying ''Night, darling' as she turns over. But he's awake, half sitting up in bed, and the glow from his reading lamp makes his face appear diabolical as he turns to her and says, mock playfully – which is the worst kind of playfully of them all – whining too, 'Aw don't go to sleep yet, honey.' He reaches across to her where she's frozen dead still, too still even for death, and tips her over slightly, so that in the mirror I can see the back of her head and one of her legs stretched out down to the floor, her tiny ankle twisting this way and that like an old woman wringing her hands. He rolls her over like a pillow so that he can get to her mouth which he kisses, holding her down with his hands, one on her head like a clamp, the other across her shoulders.

'Ah you don't want to kiss, I get the idea,' he says, then topples her right round with a big smooth movement so she's arse upwards on the bed but with her head pulled back so that I can see her face. He spits into his palm and wipes it on her, beneath the covers, then falls on her with a kind of coughing noise and I can see her eyes popping slightly at first because of the way he's hurting her and then screwed up tight with the tears still finding a way to get out and now wide open, dead calm as though she's realised I'm there and is looking right at me as he carries on, matching the rhythm of her hair brushing. I don't understand any of it at all, but I'm certain I've seen something I wasn't meant to, so I creep away on my hands and knees like a grub and go to my bedroom across the hallway, shaking like a leaf and not able to sleep all that night.

In my mind's eye, all I have is the image of her popping eyes, pale hair and then her twisting ankle pressed against the floor like it's the last sane thing she can cling to, a reassurance of something or other.

I lie there on my bed, sleepless, sweating as if in a fever, rigid with determination to understand, but in fact made nauseous with the effort of trying to stop myself from seeing that all I'm really able to do is lie there and wait for my mother to come and explain to me what the hell's going on. She doesn't come, of course she doesn't. So I wait and try to call waiting by another name. I think up stories of explanation. I invent other versions of events until I'm delirious with how many versions there are. It almost drove me crazy, listening to the voices telling stories, all as true and false as each other because all based on that one gut-twisting bafflement: what does this mean? But it enthralled me, too: being unable to talk about what I had seen had given me a taste for eloquent deceit.

Also on this night, with indelible clarity, I suddenly understood something that until that moment had been little more than an irrational anxiety: my mother already knew she was dying and my father knew it, too. So this violence, like the ghastly abnegation of her hair-brushing, was merely his way of saying that it wouldn't happen. As though filling up the last trickle of her life with his brutality could establish some rhythm that would sustain her, make it impossible for time to be curtailed by something so absurd and incomprehensible as her death.

I realise that I've been staring like a maniac at the girl's ankle because suddenly it disappears from sight and this feels like a kick in the teeth. I jolt with the sudden shock of it, almost reeling back into my seat but getting up instead, realising I have to do something. So I go down the aisle of seats and sure enough she's sitting there talking and laughing away to a young man, a good-looking bastard, which doesn't help. I shuffle about beside her, uncertain what to say, dumbstruck by the question *What right have I to ask her to come back to me anyway?* lost for words for a moment as I stand there gawping down at her, opening and closing my mouth, looking for all the world like a fish, I shouldn't wonder, and no words coming out yet.

She turns slightly, realising I'm there, looking up at me and sweet as anything says, 'Oh there you are, darling. I wondered where you'd got to. I sat down here by mistake and was just telling this man all about you.' At which point he gets up and shakes my hand – this is all true – he actually shakes my hand, and I'm too stunned to do anything. He smiles at me real polite, 'You're a very lucky man,' he utters without a trace of sarcasm. 'I wouldn't let her out of your sight again, if I were you.'

So I shake his sweaty hand and try not to look at her, because I don't know what I'd do if I caught her eye at this point, and she gets up and follows me away along the aisle, back to our seats, sitting down with a big Cheshire cat grin, calm as you please. Not laughing though, just grinning her head off, saying, 'Now will you tell me something about yourself that I can't just as well read at Hatchards?'

IV

The day is a fast, flat-iron grey now and I'm stalling for time, thinking fast, rumbling out a big easy laugh to distract her. 'Ah, but you see it doesn't quite work like that,' I tell her, letting her know how easy it is for me to patronise her. 'Everything there is to know about me you can read in the books I've written. There is nothing else.' Part of me hopes she'll swallow this line, the other half is willing her to get suspicious and notice the difference, to start to get inklings about deeper mes which, I maintain, don't in fact exist. At least, not in the way I'd be prepared to tell her about. So to lure her, I add, 'Of course, every tale reveals as much about the teller as the characters in the tale, so fiction is really a kind of warped anatomical shadow of a writer's true-life story.'

There's a moment's silence when she seems to be weighing this up, thinking it over. Then she gets lost in her thoughts, and turns to watch the cool day flow past outside, a small smile forming at the edges of her lips, upturning them slightly as she begins to laugh softly to herself like an afterthought, or as though she's remembering something.

'But then can't you tell me something you'd rather not write about? Something too awful for *words*?' she asks me, so quiet I can barely hear her. 'There must be something. Why won't you tell me? What would I do with the words once you let them out? Just a story or something that's happened, then I'll tell you whatever you want, it's all just words,' she's muttering now, fast, like someone humming a tune that gets baggy and out of shape as soon as they've gone from off the first phrase, the only one they know, the rest following on in a warm stream of pissed-away invention.

I have to lean towards her to catch what she's saying and am glad, relieved even, that she wants to hear something and that she's got the courage to ask. But I can't bear that I am so transparent to her, that she already knows I want something from her in return. It makes me want to shock her, or say anything, whatever will appal her out of that look she's got in her eyes, because there's something unnerving about her self-containment that makes my brain sweat with the sight of it. I need some distraction.

So I decide to tell her a story, hoping it'll make her react and sit still until I'm through with it, and then I can get down to eking out the stuff I want from her, as I'd intended to from the very start. *Wasn't that my original plan?* I remind myself, disgusted for a moment with my inadequacy in this present situation, shaking and stewing over a damn girl, just a girl on a train is all she is, and there are thousands like her, all of them a sure sight easier to get a story out of and that's a fact. The difficulty being to get them to keep their pretty little mouths shut, at least in my experience.

'Ah, so that's the kind of story you want to hear is it?' I say with a big smile, the last one I intend to give her until I'm through with it. 'Why, you should have said, I have plenty like that that I've never written down, not as such. You should have said straight away,' I tell her, settling more comfortably in my seat, knocking back the last of the whisky, fixing my glittering eye on her while I decide where's the best place to begin.

'I was on a train. That's how it began. It was a train pretty much like this one, really not much different at all. And the point is that it could've been this train and even this journey. It makes no difference for the purposes of the story. The land the train travelled through wasn't as important as what happened on the train, you see. Because I met someone there who told me a story which changed my life, in a way. And although this person swore it was entirely true, they also knew both sides of the tale, which made me suspect there was a degree of fabrication involved, at least at first.

'The story was about a man and woman, meeting on a train. The man loved trains, that's how the thing started. He simply couldn't get enough of them. He'd travel everywhere by train. People couldn't fathom it out about him. He'd loved them since he was very small and the love had stuck with him all his life. Well the point of it is, he would get on the train and cruise up and down to find someone he liked the look of to talk to, usually a woman, but sometimes it would be a man. This particular time it was a woman. He asked her if she minded if he sat in the empty seat opposite her and she didn't, so he sat right down and started talking to her. He'd done it hundreds of times before and this time, he assumed, would be no different.

'It was night, and the middle of winter. The train cut through the countryside and ripped its way like a thunderclap through the little stations, stopping nowhere. Express. From one city to the next. A three-hour journey. Due to arrive around midnight. The last train. It was close to Christmas, too, a bit like now, so there was that over-packed air of excitement to the journey, people not minding the mess of baggage and children as much as they usually do. He took his time with her, that was all part of his plan, because something about her eyes, a rabbity look she had, wide-eyed and trembling slightly, made him anxious for her. She looked easily scared-off and he didn't want to do that at all, at least, not before he'd found out that certain something he knew she'd have for him, that he'd want to get a hold of, take a look at and maybe carry away with him, or discard. That was all he wanted: to take a look inside her and see what was there.

'See, he was a lonely man. Jesus, was he lonely! And anxious, too, which only made it worse. It meant he couldn't escape his loneliness. He became attached to it, fearfully, as though it were a disease of the blood. So he was always checking on it, monitoring his anxious loneliness like he was tending an illness that he couldn't get to leave his body. He believed that this attachment was his salvation, his defining quality. The thing that made him who he was.

'At any rate, this loneliness was certainly the thing that spurred him on through life. So with his anxiety fuelling his loneliness, giving him an aura of burning isolation, all things considered, he thought he had found the best way to live. If not the *best* way, at least, the *right* way, the way he thought was right for him.

'He would even have described himself as a happy man, only no one asked. If they had, he would have been too anxious about it to tell them. So he kept mum and merely winkled other people's stories out of them, never the other way round, absolutely never. Only, this time, the girl's sorrowful expression moved something in him and he started to think that maybe she was a bit like him, and that maybe this time he'd take away something rare. Perhaps be able to look back on this particular train journey with a kind of affection, thinking: *that was the journey I met whoever she was and she told me whatever it's going to be etcetera.*

'Anyway, he started to look forward to her telling him her story, really anticipating what she was about to tell him in a way he hadn't done for years, and at the back of his mind he was half thinking – but really this was just a half thought at this stage, no more than that – that when she'd finished he might even quite like the idea of telling her something about himself. She struck him as the kind of person who might genuinely be interested to hear something about him, too, and this notion intrigued him: he'd never encountered it before. But he knew it was merely his own hopeful expectation that made him start thinking this way, not in fact something about her at all, really, not that.

'So there he is, sitting down opposite her. They've just swapped a few pleasant bits of conversation about themselves and he's in-breathing to ask her about herself. It's dark outside and the air around them is humming with the hundred tiny noises of muted motion which make up the lovely inside of a train carriage. The lights are flickering in a portentous way, almost frightening, like there's some kind of a storm, but they're inside and safe and everything just fine, when she turns to him before he can get in the question and says, "Let me tell you something. It's a secret. I can tell you're the kind of man who likes secrets. Am I right?" And for the first time, he's gripped by a fear like he's never known.

'*I haven't even asked her yet!* he's thinking, and this worries him, makes him suspicious. He sees the edge of control slipping away into the darkness, out of reach. It makes him shift uncomfortably in his seat, and when a train goes past close by, wham, out of nowhere, within head-snapping distance, he's overwhelmed by the sensation of time and his intention just having overlapped like a thwack to the back of his neck in the dark before his neck-hairs even get a chance to prickle up with expecting it.

'Suddenly, he is uncomfortable, like a wet eel thrown on to a bonfire, squirming and hating it. The overlapping has completely unsettled him, you see, and he's struck blind and anxious by the notion that she's going to tell him something he doesn't want to know, something about *himself*.

'And that was his problem. All the years of him travelling up and down on those blasted trains, *no one had ever told him anything which meant a damn thing to him*. Can you imagine? *Not once*. But in fact, it's perfectly possible, I reckon, to go about in that kind of charming isolation, warmly oblivious, your entire life slipping down over your head, covering your eyes like a pleasant shower and you beneath it, without a care or contact with the outside world. Perpetual pre-birth and what's so wrong with that? Or so he'd always thought, not really caring for things to be any different and, more to the point, not even able to imagine how they could be different, since by now he'd become so used to the idea of his own solitude and was glad of it like you're glad of a lousy overcoat on a cold night. So who could blame him?

'He'd heard thousands of incredible stories, ordinary stories, familiar-sounding stories, frightening stories, sad stories and he'd used all of them up – did I mention he was a writer? He'd picked them apart and taken the bits he liked the sound of, thrown away the rest, then worked them into his books. *All life is material for writing*, he was fond of saying in a pompous manner when people objected to the way he worked, irked by the way he reduced them all to a few neat phrases, a whole book sometimes, but squeezed through his own corrupting eye and puked out again. His own particular blend of puke mind you, so they had no hand in the business whatsoever. They ended up being little more than the fingers down his throat, or so they assumed, not knowing quite how much they'd got into his head and were crawling around there like ants the whole time. He probably didn't even realise this himself.

'So she started to tell him about herself, just as he'd originally wanted. Only, once she started, he wished to God she'd kept her mouth shut, or that he'd chosen someone else to leech off. But by then it was too late.

'The actual story itself, the one she told him, isn't so important. What matters: it was the story of his life. She told it as a tale divested of all the concealing patinas of glamorous half-truths and delicate little lies; all of that was stripped away. It was simply his life without any wishfulness.

' "Don't you get lonely, working always by yourself?" she asks him, not waiting for an answer, not seeming to notice the blood flooding from his face as he feels suddenly nauseous with the weight of his loneliness which, by her question, she has pointed out to him. He is like a cartoon character running on air until it sees the drop beneath it and then falls, arms madly flailing. "I get so lonely you wouldn't believe," she carries on, her eyes flickering across the dark, reflective windows of the train, the soft child-noises murmuring in the background, her voice lightly finding its place above theirs. "I got so lonely once that I killed someone," she says, giving him the warning he refuses to see, daring him to disbelieve her, he not daring to, really quaking by now as though she can read his mind. "But I love to travel by train!" she says. "I never travel any other way. Not if I can help it."

'Then she tells him about a time once, when she had sat down next to another guy she liked the look of. He struck her as the kind of person who'd have something interesting to say for himself. He was about forty, dark hair, black eyes and huge hairy hands like an ape's. It was his hands that intrigued her. It was the only thing about him she had any interest in other than his story and how it related to those hands of his. She wanted him to put them on her body so that she could see how much of her they would cover. She wanted him to spread them across her skin, mould them across her so that she could see what they would look like, the contrast of his dark hairy hands like slabs of meat or animal flesh still with the skin on, something almost dead, or at least in its death throes, spread out across her pale skin. She imagined them cold, at least, cool and dry, rough probably, too, and she couldn't keep her eyes off them. He seemed to read her mind because he took her hand while they were talking, saying something absurd about looking at her life-line and then shaking his head as he divined dark strangers she would meet, not seeming to notice the way she squirmed then in her seat, in raptures just over the way her hand looked inside his, like a pale fish, fidgeting silently, trapped absolutely.

'So imagine, there's this woman sitting there, fixated by the man's hands when all of a sudden he stands up and gives her a look and she looks at him: the sign. She follows him down the corridor and he's waiting for her like she knew he would be, in the shuddering corridor by the door to the loo. She's not so interested in fucking him as he is in fucking her, she's really only interested in his hands, which by now she is desperate to get on to her body.

'Now they're fucking away like crazy in the loo, and she's not really paying much attention to their fucking, more interested, riveted, in fact, by those huge hands like rough molten plates, fitting around her, pinning her to him just how she likes it. And all the while they're fucking, she's telling him the truth: that she does this kind of thing all the time, that this is by no means the first time, despite her rabbity, scared look, the look that had so intrigued him about her, made him want to get to know her. That actually she was only ever interested in his hands, first and foremost, and after that, in ripping out some shred of a story from him – and this is the part that bothers him the most: it's *his life* she's telling him about, holding up a mirror to his own hidden intentions.

'By now he's going fairly mad with her ravings, as you can imagine, agreeing with everything she's telling him and letting her know he agrees with her, too. But it's driving him crazy to hear his life beamed back at him like this, all the dark corners he'd rather forget about, now lit up and plain as day, even up to the admission of that one final similarity: the murder.

'At this point, though, he can barely even admit to himself that he killed someone. So, naturally, he refuses to tell her about it. He's denied it for so long that he's almost forgotten it ever happened: the chicken-necked woman on the train, limply dangling in his arms, her head weirdly cocked in his hands.

'But the way her neck intrigued him so he couldn't get it out of his mind. Jesus, that swan-like neck! It's what he has used to justify his appetite all these years: his driving need for absolution. The price is the crushing burden of that unspoken thing that's *entirely his* and also sufficient reason for his loneliness, which makes him feel isolated, like a murderer, every waking second. Yet however much he might pretend otherwise, the fact remains, there in that forgotten evening, sealed off like a dead room, finished to memory. And now the too-late overlapping of time and missed intention *bam* against the back of his neck: he's been caught out. It did happen.

'Of course, he realises this too late, poor man. Much too late. Because by then he can already feel the blade, like a rabbit-tooth kiss upon his neck. He can't blame her for it. He would've done the same thing in her position. In fact he did, remember? Just trying to find a way to edge up closer to one other human being for a while, feel the blood ebb together for a moment that's undeniable, something that would wash away the dirt of their appetites so they could both see clearly and, moreover, during the same flexing glut of time. That's all either of them wanted.'

Across the table, the girl's expression pulls me up short. She suddenly looks as though she's on the point of running off, needing to find a way out like her life depends on it, her eyes blinking rapidly, not looking at me.

'What? I thought you wanted me to tell you a story I've never written about. Well, that was it.' I say to her, a bit irritated that she hasn't told me yet what a great story it was, which it was in my opinion, and what's more, she's lucky I told it to her. 'It's true as well,' I tell her. 'I mean, I did meet someone who told me all of that, swore it was the truth. And I believed her. Why make it up? Who'd lie about being a murderess, for God's sake?'

But the girl has gone a bit pale around the gills and I wonder if I overdid it. It concerns me when women go pale. 'Are you OK?' I ask her, taking her cold little hand in mine.

'So it was a woman who told you that story?' she asks, her question an unmistakable reproach, though scared-sounding, too. 'And it's true? She really killed him in the end?'

I look at her expression, trying to fathom it out. She's half looking at me but slightly beyond my shoulder, seeing herself in the reflection of the window, I expect, as with a slam of black we lose sight of the sky and go down inside the tunnel.

V

'I doubt there's any truth in that story,' she says, with an impatient little laugh. 'And it wouldn't matter to you if there was, would it?' But her voice is full of trepidation and she's not looking directly at me yet, her shoulders angled towards the window like she's riding a bike around a bend, leaning into the curve, the speed tickling her limbs as she scrapes almost too close to the ground.

She presses her face closer to the glass, peering into the darkness of the tunnel, which flashes its regular darts of queasy yellow like birds down a coal mine, pinned to the rock face, weirdly fluttering hostages. There's nothing else to see, nor will there be, for twenty or so minutes. But she looks slightly calmer, now that the illumination from the sky is put out and we're thundering on ever deeper into this implausible hole.

From this angle, the dim lights inside the carriage slip across her throat as I watch her disappearing again so that I cannot reach her. Her head nods slightly like a delicate wind-caught flower, her fragile, tufted hair moving me to thoughts of violence. How could her hair be like that? It's absurd, and I want to tell her that. But it's not my place to say such a thing, so I keep quiet and watch her jaw's soft champ as she thinks of words that don't fit to the stuff she wants to use to cover up whatever's going on in that prettily nodding head, apparently forgetful, but I know better than that.

When she turns to me again, she has the face of someone dragged by the hair from something they were finding great pleasure in, to look, instead, upon something disagreeable. But then her nose twitches and she blinks, slowly, just once, and I realise how mistaken I am. In her eyes there's a look I shan't forget: fear. I suppose that's what you'd call it, but it's exhilaration, too.

'So,' she says softly. 'Are you going to tell me anything at all about yourself?' smirking with her lips and voice, but her eyes still aflame with that desirous terror I can't fathom. Then she lifts her shoulders up and folds her arms across her chest like an amused child, impatient for food, and she's grinning from ear to ear now but still her eyes saying something completely different to her face and body. 'Look, think of it as a bedtime story,' she says. 'We're in a bloody tunnel. It's dark. There's hardly anyone else around. Just tell me something I don't know already and then I'll tell you whatever it is you first wanted to know.' And it's unavoidable. That's what I most want from her: her guts laid out for me to take a peek at like a Greek fate-teller, muck around amongst the entrails so I can get a good look before forgetting her.

Never be fooled, once you lick the patina of loveliness off someone, there's always the creaking shoddiness to disgust you in the end, like seeing the sweating machinery at the back of a theatre when you've just sat for two hours bathed in the angelic light, your upturned baby-faced hopefulness restored to you for a time.

'You seem to be a happy kind of person,' she's saying, 'Why

don't you tell me about the time when you were happiest? That's a start. What do you say? It should be easy.'

How can I refuse her? It's true, after all, I am a happy man. So 'OK,' I say to her, spreading my hands wide on to the table, 'I'll tell you about a time when I was very happy.'

Immediately she presses her own little hands alongside mine and appears to get lost for a second, gazing at the four hands laid out on the table in front of us as though they were docile animals offering themselves as substitutes in a game of cards. I feel her skin rubbed up against mine and I like it there, my hairs whispering against the smooth moonishness of her fingers so that I have to take her hands in mine and pull her towards me across the table, getting my face close up against hers to take a proper look into her eyes, which I'm refusing to be scared by, since I intend to tell her about the time I was most happy, just like she wanted.

We sit like that, leaning slightly towards one another, her big wet eyes swallowing me up with their sadness, making me wish, for a fleeting moment – but only for a fleeting moment – that I could hunker down there with her at the bottom of that deep place she's looking up from and put my arm around her saying *shhhh* like you do to a quivering animal to get it quiet. But I stop thinking that pretty sharpish, I'm no fool.

'You see, it was a bit like this,' is how I begin. 'It's not much, so don't expect anything spectacular from it. I didn't meet the queen or get the Nobel prize or anything flashy. It was just a girl once and not that long ago either. About four years, though it feels further away than that now. It's like that with extreme happiness, don't you find? Once it's over you can't even begin to see how it could have been you, really you, acting that way and feeling those things.

'But this all comes later. First, the girl. It was simple, really. I met her by chance in the street. She asked me the way somewhere. The pavements were glowing. It was early Spring and we were in the city. She just walked up to me, before I'd taken in anything more about her than the fact that she was lovely, nothing more than that, because at the time I was preoccupied with a story I was working on and couldn't get enough space in my head freed up for girls. That's often how it is. Everything else falls away like you're wearing blinkers. But the way that she said *Is this the way to such-and-such* intrigued me: she meant more than that, I could tell, only she didn't know how to say it.

'So she asked me directions to some place in town, a cinema, I think. She said she was going to the movies later on with a friend. Anyway, I told her where she wanted to go, thinking fast while I was telling her, drawing out the directions which, in truth, were very simple. But, you see, I wanted to keep her around now that I had got her there, engaged in conversation. So I embellished the directions as much as I could while I worked out a plan and she stood there in front of me, listening to what I was telling her. But her eyes didn't meet mine, not one bit of it. They stuck like magnets to my lips. It drove me wild, watching her watching my lips like she was deaf, maybe, or fixated with the way I moved my mouth around the words. Shameless, was how it looked. I flatter myself. It was probably just her habit. In fact, I'm sure it was just her habit, as I discovered later.

'Her eyes, fixed on my lips, somehow draw me towards her own, which are moving minutely, following the pattern of what I'm saying. As you can imagine, we must've looked pretty strange under close scrutiny – both of us barely met but gawping like maniacs at one another's mouths. The point is, that I stop giving her directions and say, "Are you really in a big hurry to get to the cinema, or can I take you out for a drink? I know a place right around the corner. Let's go there."

'At this point, she quits staring at my lips and just stands there, smiling at me. Suddenly I realise that until that moment she'd had an expression of anxiety written all over her face, only I hadn't noticed until it went away. Because as soon as the anxiety has gone, her face is lit up with such radiance that I almost fall over backwards with the shock of it: joy, pure joy, blasted right across her face. That smile! It fills me up with an overwhelming urge to try to make her stay that way, lit up like that, in the street in front of me. I want to start pointing at her and yelling at the people who are passing by, oblivious – it's a busy street – I want to yell at them *Did you see that? Did you see it? It was amazing!*

'I look up at the sky real quick to see if maybe the sun just came out from the clouds, because I can't believe the way her entire aspect changed like that. But there is nothing. Only the hot white clouds, the sun hidden way back behind them where I can't see it. Anyway. I have to get hold of her somehow, so I take her arm, trying to look like I'm being merely chivalrous, getting a lovely shivering sensation of heat as she nestles her elbow up against me, her bare forearms against the thin cotton of my shirt, touching me lightly. And off we go, arm in arm, to a place I know nearby, a bar with a garden in the back where you can sit outside in the sunshine beneath a big dusty tree and drink cold beer on a perfect summer afternoon.

'That was the start of it. My happiness.

'We sat outside together, stayed there for the whole afternoon. I memorised every little bit of her that I could lay my eyes on. I couldn't believe my luck. When I went in to get us drinks I was like a madman, barging people out of the way and then almost tiptoeing back out because I couldn't believe she was real, or that if she was real, that she'd still be there when I got back.

'But there she was, sitting on the wall beneath the tree, swinging her legs like a kid, her plain white cotton dress making her look like she'd just got out of bed almost, the thin cotton of it all creased up around her knees, slender knees the size of my elbows, more or less, and one of her shoes dangling off her little foot like a promise. She had long hair, pale in the sunlight as though all the colour had been washed out of it, reflecting the white heat like a sheet of un-melting ice, dead straight and smooth to touch, too, which I did secretly at one point when she leaned past me and the sweep of it curtained across the naked skin of my face like a caress. Her body was tiny and she had strong hands, skinny fingers but with strength in them like a musician's. Big eyes, a dark golden colour like burning metal. Her eyes worried me: they were too sad for someone so lovely. But they intrigued me, and I knew that I would have to keep seeing her.

'So we sat there talking about places we'd been to and would like to go in the future, the thought *together* hanging there like a silk sash to bind us. It was perfect. Not ideal-perfect, I'm not crazy, just a wonderful time and the thing is, it went on for years. We even got married. I was happy. I was very happy. You wanted to know about a time I was happy? Well that was it.'

The girl still has her hands in mine and is looking down at them when I stop speaking. 'The next part?' she says. 'I mean, what made you really happy about her? What was it, actually?'

'Oh, it was any number of things,' I say, feeling the warm sweat seep between our pressed flesh, liking it, remembering. 'Anyway,' I go on, 'that's not the end of it, not by a long shot. The happiness, the particular kind of happiness that I had with her got lodged inside of me so I couldn't get rid of it, even if I wanted to. It was a gift. I was grateful. I wanted to thank someone but didn't know who to thank. So I thanked her. I was grateful to her. I loved her so much. I was grateful for the happiness. It was entirely because of her. I thought that without it I was nothing. And I put everything into making sure that I held it there inside me where I knew I could keep it safe.

'The thing was, that when I tried to write about it, to give her something back, like offering her a gift in return, to explain how I felt about her and how happy she made me, it was impossible. I couldn't write about it. Or, more to the point, as soon as I wrote about it I killed it. Thinking about her with all those dirty words nestled up against her straightaway turned her into someone else. I knew what I was doing and I went right on and did it. I watched her drowning with my words wrapped around her ankles, pulling her under. I was caught.

'But I didn't know what else to do to keep her. It was the reason for marrying her: to make something separate of ourselves that would last beyond the fading bodies. I had to make our attachment real and give it a life of its own so that it could live on without us, once we'd given up believing it was possible. Because I knew we would. Just as I knew she'd leave me, sooner or later, and I couldn't bear to sit around doing nothing, just waiting for that to happen. I had to do something.

'So I scrutinised her. I was attentive to everything and told myself that all I was doing was watching and recording, no more than that. And soon enough, instead of seeing her loveliness, I saw the monster. I knew that like me, she was someone equally isolated by the foul stinking life carried around inside herself, swamped for a time by happiness but in the end the stubborn life still there, bubbling away like a sewer, reminding her – me – of itself just when we thought it had gone.

'Writing her into stories, at once I saw other men's hands upon her body, eyes jellying their way across her face and lingering between her thighs like encouraged fingers. I felt gentle scratches that I wondered where she'd learnt. Not from me. I was sure, not from me. Not the way she scratched my back one night. It happened suddenly and then I saw it. Not at the time. But the next day when I sat down to write, I suddenly saw it. I saw it all. It was as though someone had scraped the thin layer of devotion off my eyeballs and there she was, hiding behind it, with countless other men crashing into her whore cunt, welcomed by her flailing thighs grappling about their backs like muscular snakes.

'I couldn't go into the street with her any more. I couldn't bear to see the men's eyes upon her. I couldn't stand to see them brush past her, their bodies slightly taller than hers so that, horizontal, they'd be fit to fuck and there'd be nothing I could do to stop that match of limb to limb. Just watch. Crouched in the darkness. Counting the sweat-drops flying as they fucked her to tears. So I watched. I watched her like a hawk, I can tell you. She was never out of my sight. I knew that I'd catch the deceitful moment and then I'd have her back inside me, the happiness and the shit of it all fitting perfectly, as it should, because at last I was seeing the truth of it.

'Anyway, then she got ill. We had been about to have children. It hadn't worked. She had to go away. There was never anything I could have done to help her. I had only wanted to make her mine. Hold on to her in some way. But I was certain of her infidelities. As certain of them as I've ever been of anything (were those dead babies even mine?). And her autonomy was too resilient. It taunted me and made me jealous. I resented the fact that she was perpetually separate from me. So I was glad that she went, that's the God's honest truth. I had been living in a state of panic for too long. I thought I'd go crazy with it. Panic and watching. My eyes hurt with it. My heart ached. I spent entire dark days certain of only one thing: that I was certain of nothing.

'I had no answers any more. It unsettled me. So she went away. And that was that. I visited the place once. It was hard for me. I had intended to go there often, to see how she was, check that she was being looked after. But in the end, when I went there, I got sidetracked, talking to some doctor or other who had been treating her. I remember walking outside on the lawn with him. I asked him to tell me how things were done there and he was keen to tell me everything, not just about my wife. So I was strolling around with him, taking it all in, not missing a thing, when suddenly I saw myself through her eyes. In fact, it actually felt as though she were watching me, her eyes upon me. I remember looking around, half expecting to see her jumping out at me from behind a tree. It scared the hell out of me. I knew that she would see my excitement as I got a hold on these new ideas, and that was the problem: even in her worst moments of suffering, my first instincts were always, and only, *to look harder*. I mean, what was I doing there if I wasn't gathering material for some tale or other? So once I'd heard all I wanted to hear, I got out of there as fast as I could and didn't look back.'

Now I'm aware of her hands again, pressing into mine as though I've just reminded her of something. She's not looking at me, so I can't see her expression but anyway I know what it will be: the eyes like two dead reproaches, over-full with things I can't even begin to affect, like wanting to change the plot in a book written two thousand years ago, when all you can do is sit there, canted over in the margins, numb with the impotence of it all. Naturally, I don't look at her eyes, don't even begin to want to. Instead, I lift my hands out from hers which cling helplessly as I move away, pretending I need to brush the hair from my forehead. It's short hair, who am I kidding?

I turn to look out of the window, knowing I can't look at her, even made uncomfortable by her reflection; not wanting to see her sweet, smiling face, her eager, bunching shoulders, nor her hot-metal golden eyes matching the slam of the tequila lights still smashing serenely past us in the lousy black tunnel, not wanting to see any of this, nor her delicate swinging ankle, carefree turning, reminding me, nor her little wrists, waiting for me to take them once more in my hands and just keep them held there so that they can be still. *I can't any more, can't do any of this*, I'm thinking, the thought spinning about like a pathetic leaf set on fire in my brain, singeing it from the inside out, the pain just getting worse, and I wish there was something, somewhere in this rotten earth, that could douse it out. But of course there isn't. What was I thinking of? Telling her a fucking story about my ever having been happy. What was I thinking? What was I hoping for? Jesus Christ.

I shut my eyes, cooling off my sweating eyeballs as best I can, keeping them shut, tight shut against the black tunnel, disturbed from this eye-silence only when I hear her go 'Oh!' A delicate sound, little more than a soft exhalation of warm breath. 'Look,' she says, 'we're out of the tunnel.' I open my eyes and she's right, we are. I can't deny it.

VI

Now we're cutting through the land again, slipping across the pale fields towards Paris, the silent slide through ice-bitten earth, past filthy farmhouses and bleached dereliction, faster than before and smoother, too, aimless eyes skimming the smoked-glass scene beyond the window.

'So you met someone. She made you happy. But then she became ill and went away. Now what?' She turns to face me when she says this, looking into my eyes as though she wants the truth. 'Are you seeing someone else?' She blushes slightly and smiles too, remembering. Thank God, it wasn't that long ago for Christ's sake.

'You see, it's like this: I'm a writer. I have a big curiosity. How could I not? That's how it is with people like me the world over. It's nothing special, just part of the job. If you don't get enough material, stimulation, or whatever you want to call it, then it's like a car running on empty, you just stop dead still, idle by the roadside, rusting, and whatever you try to do, you can't get started again. You just sit there, watching your parts clog up and eventually fall off, the whole thing wrecked, obsolete. It's no more mysterious than that, unfortunately. I mean, I wish I could pretend that it was, but why should I? It just isn't.

'And so sleeping around, feeling passion for people other than your wife, or whatever you choose to call it, whether it's with women you get to know, whores you don't, or men you didn't really want to but thought you'd better, to see how it would be – whoever it is, it is really no different from going to a strange country and getting up on top of the biggest mountain you can find and taking a look around, or lying down in the gutter and heaving in a big breath of whatever stench is particular to that region. All of it, in one way or another, if it moves you somewhere in the region of your guts, is merely rocket-fuel for writing. And believe me, you're lucky, as a writer, if you can keep on finding new tinder for your own particular dirty flame, to keep it heating up your mind, making it sweat and boil to just the right degree.

'So you say do I sleep around even though I'm married? Why do you ask me that, when you haven't asked me whether marriage made me stop travelling by train? Or going out to watch the flies in summertime? Or if I close my eyes to snow, or any number of things. Because what are bodies if not just one more bit of stuff to take a peek at, all of it the same really, for cluttering up the earth.'

'Do you think your wife ever knew what you were doing?' the girl asks now, looking down at her hands.

'No. She didn't know about any of that,' I say to her. 'There was never any need to tell her. Nor would she have minded, I think. Not really. She knew the score. She understood that I had to have some kind of privacy to be able to write. Also, it was something I could protect her from – it didn't involve her. Anyway, I always loved her. She knew that.'

'And you are sure she was unfaithful, too?' she asks, still looking down.

'Like I said,' I tell her, wishing she would get off the subject, 'as sure of that as I am of anything. I mean, it made perfect sense. How could it have been otherwise?'

She sighs deeply, her shoulders rising and falling to a heavy exhalation as she settles back into her seat, crossing her legs slowly beneath the table, fixing her eye on me, and I see the woman she was earlier resurface and fill up her limbs with a solemn sensuality that makes me feel violent: she's in control, I'm on the run.

'So is your wife better now or still sick?' She asks, her voice become deeper, deliberate with its challenge.

'She's better than she was, or so I'm told,' I say to her. 'But I don't think she'll ever be completely well. I can't imagine her ever being the same person she used to be. That doesn't seem possible, not at all.'

She weighs up this answer, assessing me, smiling, saying in a small voice, 'But why does that matter? Why does it matter whether your wife stays the same, so long as you love her. Love does not alter when alteration finds, or however it goes. And you do love her, don't you.' A statement, not a question, as though she knows me inside out and sees nothing surprising there whatsoever, and I want to mash her face against mine until she *sees* because I find her nonchalance unbearable. I want to say to her: *Don't you see? It could be the other way round, this could happen to you and then what? Then what would you do? If the one you loved disappeared like this, hidden beneath such a sickness, perhaps of your own invention, what then?*

But I don't say this to her, naturally, I just give her a look as much as to say *But you're a woman after all, how could I expect you to understand something like this, which in fact comes down to the difference between men and women,* that the love a man has for his wife is subject to different conditions: the understanding that she will not change. So that at any point of time within their coupling he can look back upon her as something unalterable, rocklike, belonging to and existing merely in a history of his own creation. *Essentially remembered,* even in the present moment. Certainly not someone to unsettle him with change. Because a man wants to know his wife and know her to be unknowable, at least different from himself, possessing some weird capacity for procreation *in his image* but never so that he will see himself *in her,* because that would mean he'd stopped, been fixed forever at her side, their altar smile like glue to bind them.

I want my look to tell her all of this, but even now she's turning away from me, barely noticing my eyes' glare like a spike in the soft part of her back, close to the knot of vital sensation. In fact, I suspect my look says nothing of the kind.

Soon the train's smooth rush across the fields is harried by a fierce whip of wind, the metal bullet of train attenuated to make a slow-motion strand of speed, something best seen from high above the land when its silent route is horrifying: there are people in there. I watch the fields, feeling her sitting there opposite me, doubting that she even looks at me. Perhaps from time to time there's the chance of eyes, but eyes that hurt and are hurt without recognition of why, like stones thrown in the dark at strangers. Suddenly she snaps her eyes wide open. 'Do you mind if I sit next to you?' she says. 'It makes me feel odd sitting here with my back turned to the direction we're going,' a sweet smile turning up the cautious edges of her mouth. 'Sure, sure,' I say, standing up so that she can get past me to the seat by the window.

So now this is how we sit. Side by side. Racing through the afternoon across the ragged French countryside and on towards Paris, her right thigh pressing softly against my knee as she settles herself more comfortably, leaning up against me like it was the most natural thing in the world, everything smoothing out into a rhythm made pleasurable by the easy silence between us.

I sit dead still, enjoying the warm weight of her head against my shoulder, her short hair like a cat's against the side of my face when I lean slightly closer towards her. 'I haven't forgotten that I owe you a story, don't worry,' she says. 'Oh, but later. Now I'm tired, worn out,' her voice subdued, almost inaudible, hot breath against my shirt as I slip my arm around her, pulling her towards me so that she can get more comfortable. She makes a small noise then, like a dog whimpering faintly in its sleep, little more than a contented out-breath, a minute exhalation. But I know its significance: she feels safe.

Her breathing finds its pattern of sleep and I keep my arm about her, holding her against me, wishing for what seems like the millionth time, that on waking everything in my life could be as it once was. But what's the use in wishing? So I stop that pretty quickly and close my eyes, appalled by the beauty of the afternoon and my situation, like this, here with her. A vague, passionate thought oozes through my mind, that if I sleep, too, then perhaps that shared tactic of implicit delay will add up to something that I can take away from here and mull over in solitude when it's all through, which I know it will be, soon enough. So I close my eyes and pretend I'm sleeping and that all of this is more substantial than it in fact is, perhaps even as much as a dream or a memory.

I remember: my wife's head against my naked chest, not unlike this, only her long, pale hair falling across my skin in a damp twist, tickling me slightly until I gathered it up, twisting it into a supple rope to hang myself by, making her laugh, her eyes dancing. The motion, then, was a boat, the engine's chug beneath us shuddering unevenly each time we smashed the waves apart through the storm, the queasy rain-smacked portholes the only source of light upon us, confusing our limbs and almost transforming us into strangers to one another. I remember the way she slept then, her cheek pressed hotly against my chest, a dead weight of trust: she trusted me with her life, is what I realised at that moment. Her head pressed against me meant precisely that and I was overwhelmed by it all, staying awake for a time to watch her body fit to mine in sleep, curved tightly against me, her legs finding their place wrapped around my own, one hand curled up beneath her chin, the other arm holding me close to her, her face smiling at first.

But she always slept badly, and soon the horrors of her dreams stabbed her into a half-sleep that disturbed me too. She was restless at that time and often woke crying, her whole body shuddering with fear. On nights like this I'd ask her 'What is it? What, my sweet?' But she'd stare at me, whispering 'Nothing,' her eyes overfull, seeing the fear in my own eyes and not wanting to add to it. *If only I'd been stronger*, I often blame myself. But what's the use? She was so often the one to comfort me when it should have been the other way round and now what can I do? Precisely nothing. So I do nothing. I did nothing. I merely watched. I was attentive to everything she did, every moment of how she was when we were together. I breathed her into me and kept her there, pulling her down to the wet centre of my lungs so that I could taste her, knowing that soon she'd be gone. The inevitability sickened me and I endlessly wished it wasn't so but still I crouched there, waiting.

Worse than all that was the excitement of it. Watching the sickness take hold of her, splintering her, overpowering her suddenly, and just as suddenly leaving her gasping, reeling, not knowing herself, but conscious of herself more acutely than most; the riddle of herself maddening her to violence, like the thick thump of a piggish jailor making you know pain until you know nothing else, then afterwards, the tenderest kiss, making her believe that bafflement was her natural state, that unease was her lot. *And you are not even who you think you are*, my books told her, which perfectly matched her stillborn sense of herself and tormented her with deceptive pangs of parturition.

But how I hated her sickness, hated myself far more for being able to watch for so long, fascinated. I watched her disintegration and then wrote about it, calling it a story, hopeful of no better alchemy than ridding myself of the oppression of loving her. Afterwards, inevitably, I was left with nothing but the grim grip of guilt. Pitiful guilt, too, the kind you expect from a damp back-street transaction, not from your wife.

She moves against me slightly, as though waking, her head

rubbing against my chest like someone trying to make a stone fit firmly in wet sand. Her left arm snakes about my waist and I feel her fingers grip and flex slightly, holding on tight as though she's afraid she'll slip. So I hold her closer and hear her murmur in her sleep, reassured.

This is how we cross the afternoon: clinging to one another. I listen to her breath and can just hear it beneath the rough hum of the engines. I stroke back the fine, tickling hair, the pale baby-covering across her perfect scalp and I try not to grind my teeth at the foulness of life and the immense stupidity of all my mistakes.

She wakes just as we approach Paris, her eyes wide as she looks up at me, smiling like someone emerging from narcotic sleep, groggy with chemicals. I kiss her forehead. It is damp like a child's as we unravel ourselves, the cold air sucked back into the shocked, empty space between us. Beyond the window, the pale city rushes faster, thicker, as we move closer towards the centre. It feels like wading upstream and I wonder what she will do when we arrive. I have no idea.

'But you mustn't feel guilty about her,' she says suddenly, casting the words aside, out of the window on to the tracks. How does she know to say such a thing? She looks at me then, someone else entirely, not the same person who only a second ago had laid her delicate, defenceless neck against my chest, trusting me. She raises her chin and there's a challenge in her eyes, no attempt at reassurance, nothing there to match her words. 'Don't you think?' she adds, waiting, suddenly impatient.

At this moment I should have got up and left. If I'd had any sense whatsoever, I should have told her *this is all too much* but instead I tell her, 'Maybe you are right. Maybe I oughtn't to feel guilty about her, though certainly I owe her something. And I'm sure we would be able to work it out now. It would be different this time, I know it.'

She merely smiles when I say that, her entire face filled up with light, laughing softly, saying 'No,' over and over, as if it's the only thing she's certain of, caressing that word like someone might caress the mashed insides of a brain with the smooth end of a hammer. Just like that. A gentle tap tap tap to reassure themselves of the easy menace of steel.

VII

When you give up hope, life holds no surprises. Just see for yourself: we get off the train together and she turns to me with a casual incline of her head. 'Are we going to stay a night in Paris?' she says. 'I'd like that. We could have fun.' As though this would be the most natural thing in all the world. The two of us, spending the night in Paris, *having fun*. In fact, at this moment, fun is the furthest thing from my mind. But the situation is hopeless, so like I said, it doesn't surprise me one bit when she says this. I draw her into a swift embrace, trying to appear light-hearted. 'Great! Let's do that.' So we let ourselves be carried along in the flooding crowd on the platform. I tell the taxi driver directions for a hotel I know that's always half empty but it's pleasant enough. I stayed there once with my wife, just before we were married, so I have my reasons for wanting to go back there.

By now it is late afternoon and the light is fading fast. Across the city and the river, the slow ebb of darkness, like the shadow of a bird's wing, is fluttering slightly, never still like the darkness in London which comes emphatically, closing out the light like a punishment. It's different here. The darkness manipulates. Read the sickish glow whichever way you like. The deception of it never fails to unsettle me, although it excites me, too, which is all part of its charm, of course.

I watch her face as we swing alongside the hotel: she appears to register nothing. She doesn't look up either, and clings to her bag, her beaming face not matching the scared fingers at all. The street stinks. By day it's a market, although apart from the stink, there is now no sign of this: everything has been cleared away and the cobbles hosed down to leave no trace, not so much as a cabbage leaf, making the stench mysterious.

She stands beside me while I check us in under one name. My own. It makes her laugh out loud and she darts for the stairs, hiding herself from view as though this were all an elaborate secret rendezvous and she mustn't be found out. 'I can't bear it!' she yelps, still laughing, though her eyes are black wells, unfathomable.

Our room faces outwards and is high up, on the corner of the building, above the place where the market will be in the morning. It has a view into the top-floor rooms of the building on the other side of the street, but no further than that. And I wonder why I never noticed this before, the claustrophobia of the place. No view, just a room. It could be anywhere. Last time I came here it was summer. I remember how my wife and I slept with the windows open, and exhausted ourselves enough not to be kept awake by the endless night-time mutterings in the street below, covering us over with their strange shapes, setting us apart from things.

We don't turn on the lights when we go inside, although it would make sense to do so, since the darkness has crept even into the unseen corners of the room and it's only possible to make out the rough square of bed, the rectangle of window. She goes into the room ahead of me and peeks out through the curtains as if expecting to be seen. I close the door softly behind me and put our bags down before going across to stand beside her, close up against her back. She leans towards me slightly when I do this, tilting her head upwards so that it fits just so beneath my jaw, and when I wrap my arms right around her shoulders she does not pull away.

We stand there like that for a long time, with nothing to watch but watching it all anyway, the noises of the street like flamboyant sights to distract us, though barely, from this absolutely right-seeming embrace. I don't know how long we stand there, unmoving, but I know I don't want it to end, although I wish it *could* end. I wish it right to my guts. But it's too late. Because looking at her now all I can see is myself, cajoled into cold focus, and that's more of a comfort than I can ever begin to say: precious reassurance that I'm not as alone as I feel, which means everything and is a world more than I deserve, believe me.

So we stand there together with me not wanting to move, but bit by bit her getting restless deep inside of herself. I can feel it happen and I'm thinking *I want that too*. But I don't know if I can, if I'm able to last beyond these moments. Because what will happen afterwards? Nothing will be any different. She'll turn from me, smiling, with that wide-eyed, blank look like hidden gold in her eyes and I won't be able to bear it. I'll be as lost as she is. But what am I doing here if I'm not prepared to risk that? So naturally, by the time her fingers reach upwards and back to touch my face, push into my hair, it's already decided. I'm just another dumb hostage to hope.

Heaven help me is my last thought before running my hands

down the length of her shuddering body, pressing her to me from head to toe, not that I'm a believer, just a hoper, which maybe amounts to the same thing in the end and *who cares* I'm yelling at my mind now which seems intent on brutalising my better judgment – which is in fact no more than instinct – and spitting on my memory like it was so much shit and not even worth that. How I hate my mind for keeping up that willowy yelping, even at a time like this, flexing its whip-snap tendrils across the fleshy part of my brain, starting up a burn that hurts, with visions of chopping off my hands and feet to let the blood pour out from the four corners of me, like I'm some kind of gory catherine wheel with her as the fulcrum spike to keep me rooted to her, while every attempt I make at movement only results in my being spun uselessly around on that one fixed point, always looking, spinning, bleeding, and if only I could stop.

But I can't stop now. So I take hold of her wrist and turn her around towards me so that I can pull her up close and pretend for a second that there's even a chance of us being able to stay like this, fixed together and with everything all right. The hope of being able to do this is enough to quench the hopelessness, and for a second I have nothing else inside my head apart from that sweet cover-up.

We fall panting to the bed, our speed of deliberate slowness forcing me to see things clearly, each thing as it happens, all of them whirring together like an out of control machine, dancing around the one thought of getting inside her, just getting in, and after that I have no further plans. Just to *get inside* where I can forget about whatever else is going on on the outside and, more to the point, forget about what might go on beyond now, even forget about myself, especially that.

I pull away from her long enough to sit up above her and take a look at her face, luminous-seeming in the sickly gloom from the street lights. In her eyes, the only thing I can recognise is curiosity, as though this is our first time. So I look away, and concentrate on the buttons running the length of her coat which is still cold from the outside, the cool air trapped amongst the fibres of the fabric like there's been a delay to time and we're still outside and all of this is going too fast, not yet involving us, so that we have the privilege of watching.

I take hold of her around her waist and scoop her up out of the coat, pushing it aside. She seems tiny, fragile and smaller than I remember: what does that mean? It makes me feel potentially brutal, so I take extra care. Her eyes are fixed on mine and she sits up so that we're facing one another, our legs tightly locked, and I can unzip her dress and lift it off over her head. We undress each other, concentrating hard, removing every bit of clothing until we are naked, never losing touch with each other's bodies as though this were some kind of solemn game. Winning means the final struggle beneath the tight-stretched white sheets so that we can lie together, length to length, momentarily like practising children until we get permission to move, dead still, almost, until that moment and then everything else abandoned to the wordless search for one another's pleasure – at least, the attempt to loosen the threat of pain and unrest which now thunders like the shadow of a storm above us until we find a way out. And *fighting my way further in* is the only way out, I'm convincing myself, this idea urging me on like fire at my back, so that I'm standing on the burning deck with the ocean black and dreadful around me, and no other living thing, or shape of a thing of any kind on the horizon, nothing, just the flames' grotesquely licking tongues, fast putrefying my flesh. Should I jump? Now? Or wait until there's at least a ship on the horizon. Or at least a sign of someone else aboard who can tell me what to do.

But there is no one. Only her. And she has already sunk to the mermaid bottom, long, long ago. Deliberately sunk to sing me downwards into the darkness with hot breathing wetness to drown me and make me think it's something other than dying.

I grip her shoulders hard. I can feel the shape of her bones beneath the skin and flesh. They feel unbearably frail and I know how easy it would be for me to grip harder and crush them, splinter them so that the delicate spikes would stick out through her skin like a secret sea creature's tiny spines. I hate her for her weakness. I know she couldn't hurt me in the same way. This thought depresses me and makes me look away, shutting my eyes tightly as I go inside her, hearing her groan, a shudder of pain as though I'm hurting her right through to her guts and I'm glad of that sound, wanting to grip her harder. So then I do grip her harder and she cries out, her wild eyes sudden with fear, leaping beyond suspicion to see the truth: *I want to hurt her for not knowing me yet.* I look into her eyes to see if there's any glimmer, the slightest glimmer of recognition would do, but there is nothing for me to cling to. I have to settle for her fear. So I rip it out of her eyes and suck it into me where I can feel it, wanting to flip her fear over on to its belly so I don't have to face the risk of procreation, duplications of terror, more monsters to remind me of myself and how much I have failed her. I stare hard. But I know that however hard I stare, I'll see nothing. She can give me nothing.

I sink myself into her, boring into her like a deep-sea diver's bad dream of rock, everything wrong, the wrong order, just the nightmarish mix-up of habit and desire. It's the certainty of failure that keeps me going. And something else. I see it in her eyes, beaming back at me like an insane lighthouse already ten thousand miles beneath the waves, fooling sailors with a jaunty flash of misleading light, deliberately wrecking the matchstick boats. It's there in her eyes. Suddenly. Then gone. And there again. Some glint almost of recognition as I surge into her, both of us awash with sweat like the ocean, fighting and staring hard enough to make our eyes burst out of their jellied delicacy; while I screw myself into her and she goads me on like she's seen it, too, the light reflected back in my eyes as I'm willing her to know who the hell I am because she's not quite there yet despite my silent bellowing.

But in truth there is no recognition, and the eloquence of my flesh cannot be heard. It is as though the words that soar around me, screaming from my eyes, are in fact whispered, some centuries ago, on the other side of the world, by a madman in a foreign language, or at any rate a language unknown to her. Or maybe the words were never even spoken but merely written down, once, alone in the night, and the book instantly burnt, the whole thing unbelievably difficult even to get a glimpse of from where we are now.

And I wish like a fucking numbskull's prayer that she could *see*. But she doesn't, and I'm right there on the edge now and so is she. So we're suddenly like two speeding satellites on different trajectories with the sun flashing off us both at once and then leaving us as we fall down, shaded by the earth, signifying nothing beyond that final demise. My eyes have a pathetic last demand: *know me, for crying out loud, know me!* That's how it must look, merely an invocation, something dog-like, that's all. But when I look into her eyes there is nothing, just the perfect sphere of golden gristle, the neat iris ripe for slicing.

So what it comes down to is that I'm probably no more than mistaken. Mistaken about her, and in thinking that there was a chance for us. This is what I'm realising as we reach our little deaths together, both of us concentrating on the simple grind of flesh. Seeing the end and finding it with the ease of instinct, our bodies knowing how to do this only too well. We peel apart, dripping sweat, gasping for air. I stare up at the ceiling, trying to replace the sight of her empty eyes with a vision of wallpaper that is obscenely similar: it too tells me nothing.

'Are you OK?' she asks me casually from another planet, her inquisitive fingers touching me softly on the top of my head like a blessing. I turn on to my side to face her, pulling her over so that I can see her better, still hopeful for that look which doesn't exist. 'Of course. Are you alright?' I search her face, humiliated by her blushes and concern. 'Yes,' is all she says, looking up at me, her fingers stroking my hair in a dreadful simulacrum of understanding. Mirroring her, I twist the tiny lengths of her kittenish hair between my fingers, touching the delicate strands at the nape of her neck, running my hands along her back, drawing her closer, wanting her again. For a moment, I lose sight of my own black guilt, forgetting the horror of her distance from me as I move inside her like a slow kiss, wanting only to calm her poor troubled brain, which I now see is burning with something unstoppable that I will never understand. This time, she closes her eyes, and I imagine the relief she might find in darkness.

It is evening by the time we go outside and the cold shocks us closer together, clutching at the heat of our bodies. The streets are almost deserted. Voices are subdued as in an empty school outside of term-time. It feels as though everyone has left the city for Christmas, or else they are all hiding inside their houses like children, not wanting to be heard. Walking beside one another like this, our arms tightly curled around each other's bodies, I can feel myself staggering slightly, trembling with the unexpectedness of the last few hours. I think *I have no idea what is running through her mind, none whatsoever.* I want to protect her, although I know I can't, that her demons are strangers to me and I have no control of them. We walk the long way round, heading towards the river. On the bridge, dead centre, we lean against the parapet looking towards the yellow-lit church on the hill and I imagine that we fit into someone else's story for a time. All this beauty.

We stand there for a moment, our noses burning with frost. I watch the grind of water gnaw the surface of the river from beneath. Then, softly, I hear her swearing at herself. A delicate obscenity, touching despair with the tip of her tongue. I pull her back towards me, tug her sharply close up against me, suddenly having a vision of her trying to get away, throw herself off the bridge, seeing her do it with impotent clarity.

'It's fucking freezing out here,' I say. 'Let's go and eat. Aren't you starving?' And she looks up at me, seeing what I'm trying to do for her, watching the effort of will I'm trying to swamp her with, to bring her round and out of this lousy pit of anguish she's just about to leap into, arms flailing, laughing with that casual laugh I know she's on the brink of, almost as though I can hear it bubbling up inside her, and believe me it terrifies me half out of my mind. So I'm glad to the point of almost whooping with it when she pushes herself tighter against me, saying 'Oh yes, yes, that's such a good idea. Why are we standing here? It's so cold. Let's eat. Let's do that.' And we walk off that bridge as if chased by harpies, or at least chased away by that vision of her standing on the parapet, arms windmilling, leaping into the dead water with a glad intention, absolutely careless.

Once off the bridge she looks at me with a grateful smile, so I think *now we're getting somewhere, this is better*. 'You're going to be OK kiddo,' I say to her and she smiles back at me as though she knows what I mean. So then off we go, arm in arm like a regular Paris couple, away along the river bank towards a restaurant I know just around the corner.

It is evening and the city looks incredibly lovely. The strings of coloured lights, the wet boulevards glistening like ancient whalebacks, the secret colonnades, the brackish mirrors reflecting crowded cafés, incurious people passing by, demonstrating the appropriate way to behave. We walk through it all, watching our four feet swing along beneath us, naming things to one another as we pass them, using all the right words, rounding the corner to the restaurant. I open the door for her, holding it so that she can go in ahead of me as I turn back to take a look at the street before we go inside. And it's undeniable, everything seems just fine.

VIII

O f course this doesn't last. But even I'm caught out by the speed at which things start to break apart.

We sit down at a table by the window and get busy ordering food, choosing wine, talking in hushed tones about the people in the restaurant, the ones passing by outside. The familiar kind of chatter that can so quickly establish a pleasant rhythm of numb ease between couples, setting them apart from others with perfect legitimacy, little islands of hope. I can see how easy it is to be like that. All it takes is two complicit people and the appropriate setting. *Take a look, we're doing it ourselves right now* I'm thinking. *It's so easy that even we can do it.* Although this is so far from the truth I could weep, and half expect applause at moments of particular conviction.

Yet we perform our parts well. From time to time, I'm almost able to lose my reason in some candle-lit reverie, pretending that our meticulous charade can last and, linking up to time in this manner, perhaps even become real.

So naturally I think nothing of it when, during a break in the meal, she excuses herself and gets up from the table, 'I won't be long.' Only then the minutes stretch out and there's no sign of her. The thump of suspicion starts weighing against the back of my neck which feels like it might break with the effort of not looking round to see where she's got to. I pull the sleeve of my shirt down further over my watch so that I don't have to look at the hands spinning relentlessly round the dial, taunting me. *Where is she?*

'She's not well,' I tell the *maître d'* who hovers uncomfortably, discussing the situation with one of the waiters. I feel sorry for them. This kind of thing must happen all the time. They are probably bored by its inevitability. I expect they've seen it a thousand times. But I despise myself for being so readily anxious, humiliated by my burgeoning feeling of panic and cowed by it, too.

I stare at the food and hate it. I look out of the window and see nothing but the vileness of strangers. All beauty gone now. My hands, clutching the weird knife and fork, look ambiguous with violence and impotence. I loathe them for it. They appear obscenely malevolent and threatening. Everything seems suddenly pointless and stripped of all meaning. I see my hunched body reflected in the windowpane and there's nothing in the sight to comfort me. I see only a pile of bones, the hot wine flush distorting the gnarl of lips and the eye-pits like shitholes in hell.

I tell myself that this is a sign. That her going off like this, without explanation, making me wait, is the final sign I need. I should just leave, that must be what she wants me to do. And maybe that's what she's done herself? Crept out the side door while my back was turned? She has every reason to do that. Things are over between us, run their course, finito, kaput. So why am I hanging around? It's unlike me to be persistent. I should just let go and start over, accept defeat and move on.

The waiter slides past me on oiled wheels, a subtle incline of his head as I tell him, 'She won't be back.' His hands flicker across her untouched plate and then the whole thing is swept away. Her glass, cutlery, all gone, the chair pushed in as though she were never even there. I think of widows remarrying too soon and laugh softly to myself. How easy to eliminate someone from your life. I'm becoming an expert in it and now this lovely waiter's discreet flourish *voila!* and that's the end of her. I laugh out loud, throwing my head back and bellowing into the dark restaurant like a sore-bellied fool, hating so hard that my sides start to ache with it.

By the time I stop laughing my appetite has vanished and I feel guilty, looking at the effort congealing on my plate. I'm overwhelmed by the need to get away, so I make a great show of rolling up my sleeve to take a squint at my watch, exclaiming surprise, the whole works, as I call for the check.

Looking at the place where she sat makes me grind my teeth, maddened by myself and wishing I could lose my skin, or at least clean it, because it's there that my memory lies tonight. Still stinking of her particular sweet skin smell, my cock still glistening with her and my heart still pounding with the effort of pretending. I've become an enemy to myself.

To forget her, I'd have to flay myself, I realise quietly, smiling a tiny smile like a shark might, surreptitiously. To rid myself of her, I'd have to take a fine slice off every surface of me, including my brain, guts, pineal gland, spleen, lungs, liver, heart and all the rest of the filthy heap of meat. Then I might stand a chance. Otherwise, I'm a dead man. And still the struggle, that's the remarkable thing. It fills me with a certain degree of pride, I admit, that despite the absurdity of my not being able to rid myself of her, still I struggle: wading in, or wading out, at least it's some attempt at movement, even if I lost sight of the light above the skin of the sea a long time ago.

Only there's her empty place-setting like a reproach, as though by having it cleared away, I've eliminated all chance of her coming back. It's so clean. They even shaved it with a knife, scraping imaginary crumbs from off the erased linen like maniacs. Should I care that they did that? Jesus.

But the emptiness of it. *Where the hell is she?* It feels like she's been gone for hours. I fantasise hotly for a moment that she never even happened. The thought fills me with ecstatic terror, so I stop doing that pretty quick.

I shut my eyes for a minute and, unbidden, I remember the day she went away before. The pitiful efficiency with which I cleared her out of my life, yakking on to whoever would listen about how it was destroying me to see her suffer like that, really it was, that professional care was the only solution, watching the bovine nod of their heads as they agreed with me, *sorry for what I'd been put through*, for crying out loud. They came for her when the wind was up and screaming through the treetops in the square. I flew to New York the same day and caught up with some old friends. I went out drinking that night. 'Oh sure, my wife's fine,' I'd say when they asked, making them laugh and grin with cheerful admiration at the way I went home with the girl in the biker boots before closing time. An easy declaration of independence: *see, I still do what I like, marriage hasn't changed me.*

Back in England, meanwhile, the screeching wind, the dark blue car curving round the bend in the road, the insane rooks thrown like black hangman's hoods into the sky and shot down with arrows, wildly plummeting but without weight, scaring me out of my mind. I was reminded of rats and airborne fear: fear can float, you see, be carried on the air like a wish. I averted my eyes and went back inside the house before the car was out of sight, packing up my things as I walked through the hallway, plucking my passport from its usual perch on top of the notice board, put there for that very reason. Take one in case of emergency. I always had to have a way out.

Earlier that same afternoon there was sunshine. The year was dying but the sun shone and made me glad. I was fixated by it. It told me all I needed to know: things would go on. What more did I need than that reassurance? We took a walk together, through the park and over to the lake where the children's boats bucked amongst the little waves and the water darkened and glittered mysteriously as the wind caught it. The whole world was restless, is how it seemed. The trees shook and people bent weirdly as they walked, putting their shoulders to the wind like coal merchants. She walked apart from me and always danced out of reach when I tried to catch her, staring at me malevolently, her eyes brimming with menace: *it's all your fault*, I thought they said at the time, although later I saw things differently.

The one moment I did manage to grapple her against me was from simple necessity. She strolled towards the lake with ecstasy scored like light across her upturned face. Her arms moved across her body like a lover's, twining themselves hotly about her, running up her sides, one of them twisting into her pale hair which whipped about her body, a riot of anaemic

snakes, dancing as though beneath the sea during an earthquake, the water boiling around her tiny skull, the threat of
unseen rocks to bruise her brain. I knew she wanted to crawl
along the bottom of the lake and open her eyes to the newness
of drowning, but by the time she broke into a run, leaping
towards the water's edge, I was already beside her, pulling her
up against me, wrestling her to myself, shocked by her strength
and more shocked by the venom in her eyes when I shook her
hard, yelling 'No' until she was still.

But not before she'd bitten hard into my shoulder, drawing
blood, her eyes full of hate and not knowing why I'd stopped
her, though certainly hating me for doing it. And then, once
she was quiet, I gripped her arm in mine, linking her to me, and
we walked across the brow of the hill, commenting on the kites
as though nothing had happened. In fact, for her, nothing *had*
happened and she was already a different person with no flicker
of recognition as she looked down at the black lake. It held no
charm for her now. That was someone else's life. Moreover,
someone whom she had never set eyes on before. I was beyond
protecting her. So we simply walked and then returned home,
taking no notice of anything.

I sat beside the window when they came. She sat opposite me
in her coat, plucking off her gloves and replacing them fast, the
sight of her hands seeming to unnerve her, her suitcases waiting
in the hall. She smiled the whole time. A smile from the pit of
hell with no sense to it whatsoever. Unless a memory, written
down and pinned against someone's naked throat with a razor
blade makes any sense. *And perhaps it does*, I'm thinking as I look
at that smile and those unfettered eyes which see every damn

thing stripped to their stinking bones and then more, right down to the useless marrow and aching gristle, God help her. So we sat there, eyeing one another like apes until they came to take her away and I let them, helping them do it, showing them to the door once they'd got her. There was no struggle.

And when she left, she took my arm as though I were the one who was ill, saying 'You'll be OK, darling. I promise. I know you're going to be fine. Just don't look so worried.' Then letting go her hold on me like an indifferent relative, she raised her hand in farewell, a brief, delicately waving gesture as though she were trying to remember something, perhaps, and anyway not too bothered to remember, and then forgetting even that there ever was anything she'd forgotten. Just a slight sweep of the air like someone conducting a phrase of silence for an absent orchestra. She smiled too, though not at me, as she got into the back of the car, unresisting.

It was all my fault. I made it happen then, and now it's just the same. I open my eyes and stare hard at the empty space ahead of me, trying to think of nothing but the angle of the chair in relation to the table, the table in relation to the window, the way the mournful flower droops in the cheap vase, the grain on the wooden seat of the chair, probably still warm from her lovely arse. I can't bear it a second longer. The check is in front of me. I sign it and go, almost running from the restaurant.

Outside, the cold is miraculous against my face. I want to lick it, it feels so good. Once I've got a few streets away, I stop, out of breath. Leaning against a doorway, I squint up at the sky and there are even stars. *So things can't be that bad*, I tell myself. I shut my eyes to it all and start walking in the direction of the hotel, agreeing with myself that of course I'm not thinking about her. That's it. She's gone.

The city seems deserted. I see almost no one. But in the cafés the world still exists and passing by the bright windows feels like walking along a treadmill of someone else's life, a perpetual spectator, everything going on behind glass, leaving me utterly uninvolved.

I find this reassuring. And as I walk, soon enough, I start to feel almost roguish, staggering back through the night, contemplating whores. At one particular café window I prop myself up against a lamppost and piss into the gutter, watching the bright arc of pee golden-curving across the light from the windows. I grin to myself, sighing with relief, glancing across to the window to see if anyone has noticed. The café is quite empty and I don't focus too well on the people standing at the bar or lurking in the corners, multiplied by the mirrors.

Only one couple catches my eye. It is her, I swear it, sitting in the window with a man. I blink hard and try to straighten out my eyes, pissing on my foot as I turn around to get a better look, cursing, putting my stupid cock away fast and getting behind the lamppost so she doesn't see me watching her. I'm outraged. Now what's she playing at? But I'm fascinated, too, and want to see what she does.

Leaning towards the man opposite her, she appears to hang on his every word, her lips trembling expectantly, and I wonder why she's taken so long about it and doesn't just take him off and fuck him right now, she seems so desperate for him. Her fingers dawdle lazily over the stem of her glass of brandy, a suggestive touch that it's straightforward enough to interpret.

From time to time she touches her hair, as though forgetting that it is shorn like a baby's, so that she has to touch it to remind herself. The man is a surprise: he looks just like me. Late thirties, dark, heavily built, sure of himself. He eyes her with an expression of undisguised glee as though he can't believe his luck. Though if only he knew the truth he wouldn't feel so lucky. I'm on the point of telling him, just walking in there and saying, 'Get out while you can. She's crazy as hell. She'll ruin your life. She'll fuck you up.' That kind of line. Though obviously I do no such thing. Far better to watch and learn, which is what I do.

But not for long, because all of a sudden she turns to look out of the window as though suspecting that someone is lurking there. Her eyes beam across to me but register nothing, although she must have seen me because the skinny streetlamp is no great hiding-place. So there she is, looking straight at me. And instead of creeping away, or sinking back further into the shadow, I move out further into the light as much as to say: *Yes, it's me. What did you expect? I'm not stupid. Of course I'd find you out.* But the look in her eyes shocks me. Irritation, is all it is. Nothing more than that. As though I'm her father come to collect her too soon from a school dance when she'd just lined up the boy she wanted, and now I've come along to spoil everything, ruin all her fun. For Christ's sake, I think, I'm not cut out for this, it's hopeless, he's welcome to her. So I stand there, beneath the street light, swaying slightly no doubt and in full view, until she turns again to her beau and gives him her full attention, never once looking back outside at me.

I feel absurd, spying on her little liaison like a madman. So I turn on my heel, taking one final peek before I hotfoot it out of there. Her hands are touching some invisible thing in the region of his eyebrows, maybe temples, the point being that this gives him an excuse to take a hold of her hand and kiss it – the same hand that only moments, or maybe hours ago, I had had all folded up inside my mouth, the better to taste her flesh. So he's kissing her hand as I leave, then drawing her towards him across the table so he can kiss her lips, too, and she is unresisting. In fact, she is swamping him with the heat of her kisses. I can see her doing this, plain as day. There's no doubting what she's up to. My one kick against the building, numbing my foot to match my heart, is irrelevant to the point of being ludicrous. This is not hurt. What I'm feeling is something between disbelief and horror. A black place with the world's weight upon it, where each person is fixed in sordid isolation, never glimpsing another living soul but knowing they're there. Unseen. Without even the chance of eyes, though possibly the twisting touch of clever fingertips on steel – midnight's fatal pulverisation. This is where I am now, as I stagger alone through the streets, wishing I were someplace else entirely, preferably another world or time.

I walk away. But in my mind's eye I see her still, caught up in the infernal embrace, behind glass like an unobtainable fish with me as the nasty, itchy-pawed cat, stalking around forever on the outside, a complete fool, starting sincerely to doubt my sanity like a dead man doubts life. But like I said, this is what I do best: observe, move on, take note, be attentive to everything. It's my job after all. So what else can I do?

I arrive at the hotel around three. The room is empty and she hasn't been back, according to the evidence of the undisturbed bed. I undress, wondering, as I always do, why I got so drunk. As I crawl under the sheets, I tell myself that this is perfect, really more perfect than I could have hoped for. She's made the decision for me and now I'm free of her. I decide that tomorrow I will simply pack, leave on the first train out, and be sure as hell never to let her find her way back into my life. This is the absolute end of it for us. I lie there, watching the ceiling, the gangrenous flicker from the street lights, the whole sorry scene, all of it glossed over with the stink of our bodies from that afternoon, the sheets reeking of her delicate stench that I can't help but adore, can't even begin to kid myself that I'm not inhaling deeply, trying to fill my lungs up with it. *Where's the harm in that?* I ask myself, breathing like a drowning man getting his final nicotine fix of salt water.

So I lie there, watching the night become dawn become morning, sleepless, despite the alcohol. Still, she doesn't come back. I stare at the door, trying to imagine her blazing through it with apologies and denials, offering excuses for the way she left me sitting there like an idiot in that damn restaurant last night. But with every second that passes, it gets harder to summon up that image. Each time I try to imagine what she would say, all I can see is her lovely face, and a question in her eyes: what am I doing to her? That is the vision I have, strengthening with each wakeful moment. And as the light brightens along the crevice between the curtains, with the booze leaving my veins in a slow tide of remorse, I have to admit my guilt.

It was me who left that restaurant, not her. Of course it wasn't her. She had probably only been gone for a few minutes, but straight away I saw those minutes multiplying into an entire future without her and I couldn't bear it, couldn't stand to sit there, powerless, waiting for her to come back. Such neediness appalled me. Better to leave immediately while I could still feel the insult of her kindness and trust, which felt like the worst kind of blame: she had no reason to trust me, as I soon enough proved.

But maybe it's not entirely my fault? After all, where did she get to last night? Perhaps she had wanted to find a way out, too? But I know that's not true. I saw my chance and I took it, leaving her to the night. I was certain she wouldn't be able to find her way back to the hotel.

Now I know it will be over. She cannot forgive me for this and I don't want her to, can't bear to be given so many extra chances. I stare at the door and can't even conjure up a fantasy of her guilt any more. All the treachery is mine.

So when it's a reasonable *What the hell's reasonable?* hour to get up, then up I get, have a bath, shave, dress, all the usual things, pack my case, getting ready to leave. At the door, looking back into the room, I ask myself: am I a changed man? Have these last twelve hours changed me?

I don't know the answer. But I suspect it. And I'm disgusted with myself for having for so long been dead to what my own guts are telling me. But now I have no choice. She's gone. And besides, I was the one who drove her crazy and more importantly, *away*. This is only as much as I deserve.

IX

I leave the hotel, thinking *Never again. I'll start over. Make a clean break. I'll just have to forget about her, because what's the alternative?* It doesn't even bear thinking about. So I try not to think at all.

Outside in the street, the market is in full swing and the lovely pong of vegetables distracts me for a moment as I walk through to boulevard St Germain. A wind has started to burn through the city and when I stop to look up at the sky, the clouds appear unnaturally fast, making me feel sluggish, and I wonder how easy it would be for me to stay like this. Just watching things, never trying to reshape them or say they might have happened a different way. But I can't help wondering where she is. Nor can I pretend that I don't feel foolish, humiliated by my blatant dependency.

I start to walk, sneaking looks up at the racing sky from time to time, pretending to myself that I'm merely taking a stroll on an ordinary morning and not thinking about her at all. I walk past the restaurant where I left her last night. At the same table, two young girls are hotly debating something secret, their silent hands clutching pieces from out of the air between them until they suddenly break apart, laughing. One of them glances out of the window, sees me and smiles, saying something to the other, more laughter as they try not to point at me and pour their guts out into the street with mirth.

I'm a laughing stock, I tell myself, made ridiculous by my wife even when she's gone. Look at me, for God's sake. I disgust myself. The fact that this is nothing unusual repels me even more. Just another person oppressed by guilt and the weight of their own private, long-held fixation which they at last suspect is no more than a mistake. But I don't budge an inch from that spot until they've quit looking at me. I have some pride left. So I pretend I'm trying to find something in my bag, not gawping at the place where she was at all. Then I get the hell out of there.

People's faces depress me. I'm sickened by the thought that I can't know every one of them. More sickened still by the thought that I don't care to know any of them, apart, of course, from that one elusive face which is branded on to my mind's eye like hot lead, congealed into her image. It's not love, just an impression, I say to myself, lying. I feel violent when people touch me in the street. I don't really look out for her for the simple reason: I don't expect to see her again. But I do look. I look so hard my eyes start to smart.

I was never any help to her. Never any use whatsoever. I kept trying, I now suspect, merely through the force of inertia, my heart like a stone set in motion on a perpetual incline, always rolling, never at rest. It's all I am, I tell myself, a uselessly rolling lump of inert dread.

I only ever wanted to drag her along with me. Use her for food in a way that she might have found some pleasure in the consummation, too. That's all it ever was. It was never my intention to damage her in a way unfixable. I hoped she'd be able to see my use of her as a compliment, if she ever chanced to reflect upon it, which I hoped she would not. Was such a misconception possible?

To realise my mistake, I only have to look at her. Be attentive to how she is. Then I can see her sink beneath the darkness I once called invention. Pitifully helpless and not pretending otherwise. Merely overwhelmed by the chemicals hotly brewing in her brain and so giving up the fight. And how could she have fought, with me denying her the fact of battle? 'It isn't so,' I used to insist, driving her out, 'This isn't you. That's not me. Of course not. You are real. This is fiction.'

I curse myself softly under my breath and keep walking, with the sky tearing along overhead, the people scurrying like rats and me one of them, the biggest rat of them all, and the only thing I want for myself now is to be free of it. Free of the scum of memory. The shit of needfulness. The crap of dependency and want, wishing the whole world and me in it would explode and rearrange itself in an order entirely different from how it in fact is: the moronic drudgery of scepticism and separation.

I walk faster, hitching my bag over my shoulder, bearing down on people like a lunatic, making them scatter. I'm incensed by the futility of every damn thing I can imagine and all the things I can't, all of it made worthless for being no more than my own dim imaginings. For what else could it be?

If I breathe deeply, I can smell my brain rotting, for sure I can. There are maggots, too, somewhere in the mess of writhing offal, just beginning to poke their little heads above the rim of mush. To be oppressed by such a thing exhausts me.

I dream of the surreptitious cut and slice that would remove this thumping grey rubbish from my head, take it out so I could get a few laughs from it, watching it shudder and burp on the operating table beside me. It calms me somewhat to know that I have such an easy way out available to me, if only my sides would stand it – the hysterical laugh afterwards. There's a cure for everything but not for this unalterable fact of isolation: every man *is* an island, whatever they say. But more isolated even than that, with not even any sea to bind them. Just illusions of sea. Delightful illusions of oceans. The viscous tread across the water towards another person something magical, and entirely impossible, too, which is the main thing.

My shoulders ache. I want to stop but I suspect that if I do, I'll roll into the gutter and weep like a hungry snake, overwhelmed by this mongoose fantasy of unity and communication that burns at my back, goading me on to walk faster and further, searching for food. *This is my hell*, I know now for sure, and it's a place of my own making. I sniff scents of exquisite nourishment, but as though with my hands, feet and mouth cut off and thrown away, so *all* I can do is smell. And at the end, now, I am thrown out into the blazing desert and asked, *Did you like that? Would you like some more? First though, explain precisely how it was, don't forget a thing or leave out any detail.*

So then the words flood out, mainlining outwards from my heart, cooling my sweating brain for a while. And it's only a matter of time before I start to feel the free-fall anguish of isolation transform itself: the momentum of going down fast and alone sends sparks flying off me when only a short while ago I was shit-wading like a slow buffoon. This always happens.

I'm lucky that way. It's the suspicion that it won't happen which drives me wild with fear. It's the pre-horror fear that oppresses me the most. Like staring at the sun until your eyes burst into flames. Mere sight is painful until that moment of release. Only then is it worth something, as your phoenix eyeballs plummet earthwards with a screeching speed that is pure euphoria.

I walk some more and it seems to me that with each step I take I'm burning more provocatively, not moving through the city so much as *moving*, the motion itself become the edging-on into the guts of darkness, so that all false feeling of connection to the light and *her* glitters off behind me like moonbeams at night, disintegrating wildly beneath the skin of the sea. I think: soon I'll be empty of everything, a preposterous void walking through the world.

I walk faster, not anticipating, exactly, but still alert for that deluge of emptiness, almost palpable, as it shuffles in readiness around me: the crushing menace of brute facts, from the stones beneath my feet to the bouncing blue hitting my retina just so, firing up the illusion so that I can live by it for these particular moments.

I think again of when my wife went away before. The violent wind, flapping trees, a scene much like today. Cold air chewing my face as I slammed the front door and raced to the airport as though my life depended on it. On the edge of my seat in the taxi, cursing the driver for the traffic, desperate to escape, leaping like a criminal on to the first flight out of London. Even airborne I was anxious, still echoing with the anguish of her going away. I blamed her. It was easier to blame her than myself. She left me, didn't she? She was the weak one, the one to get sick, not me. But still, she wasn't so weak that she didn't have the strength to leave. I raged against her for doing that to me. For humiliating me in that way. Stripping me naked and leaving me panting like a dog for her while she got into the car and left, just one curve in the road and she was gone, deliberately tormenting me with her clear-sightedness and undead affection, despite everything.

But the thought I cling to is the quick exhilaration of being without her. I fought like a beast to make myself feel it as soon as possible after she left. It was surprisingly easy. All I had to do was get away, always away. Cut loose and keep moving. Remind myself that that is the right way to live. And not be bothered, not if I can help it, by the image of life as nothing more than enervated excrement, fizzing with the heat of its own decomposition. But now, for the second time, here she is, walking out on me and here's me feeling aggravated by it. *Not so fast*, I tell myself, *I'm leaving first this time*. Of course, that much is undeniable. Then why do I still feel betrayed to my guts by her? Mad as hell at her, too, for denying me a fight to the death to finish things off once and for all. But I try to push this thought from my head and keep walking.

The sun comes out, so I keep to the shadows, my polite eyes averted from the whole sordid scene, not wanting to watch it for a moment longer than I have to. My feet ache and my shoulder burns where the strap of the bag has gnawed into my skin. I detest my delicate flesh.

It's time I got to the station, so this is where I go, hailing a taxi on the next intersection, suddenly desperate to get out of this idiotic city on the cusp of celebration. It's better inside the car. Not only better on my feet and shoulders but more pleasant to see things from behind the cage of glass. People on the pavements swim by harmlessly and I think *Soon I'll be rid of the entire stinking lot and back on the lovely train, then out of here.*

I arrive at Montparnasse with a few minutes to spare. Beneath the piss-fragranced vaults, the crowds of people heave and stagger as though as eager as I am to get out of the city. Walking into the station overwhelms me. It is a homecoming. Relief at being here, just someplace where there are trains, eases me straight into a state of calm excitement that is close to serenity. I look about me and my eyes feel cool, all the heat suddenly washed out of them.

I stand still for a moment, reading the numbers and names off the huge information panel. All the places I could go to. It would make no difference. Any one of those places would do now. I could just slip into someone else's life, or spend my days in complete solitude, stepping off the train with my eyes tight shut, taking pot luck and seeing how it felt. Of course, I have no intention of doing this but the thought that it is even possible thrills me. Choice is a great creator of illusion: in this case, the illusion of self-control.

I scan the crowds, admitting to myself that I'm looking for her. Where's the harm in that? And she could be here. It is possible. Because what if she finds that piece of paper they gave her at the hospital? The one which gives details of the train she arrived on yesterday, and the train she was supposed to take today, what time, which station – but by then she'll probably have already missed it, of course. She'll scrutinise that little piece of paper, turning it over and over in her hands, utterly perplexed, with no clue as to why she was going to take the train or even whether it was she who was supposed to take it. I know the look she will wear upon her face at that moment, her forehead wrinkled with a fierce cleft between her eyebrows, her wide mouth pouting like a petulant child as she clings to the scrap of paper, utterly mystified, and angry with herself for being mystified. In a fit of rage, she'll scrunch the paper up and throw it into the bin, instantly forgetting it, then get dressed, go out, slip into some other life, any number of things, all of which I am now powerless to affect, having given up on her. Which is what I have done, I remind myself, taking one final look around the station concourse before heading over to the platform.

I get on the train and tell myself that what I am feeling is pure relief that she is not here. I hold my breath while the doors suck closed and the train starts rolling forwards, slipping out of the station and on into the bright day, now luminous with frost. This is it, I tell myself portentously, this is what is called the start of a new journey. See how easy it is.

I watch the city speed up alongside the window, the gleaming grey unlike anywhere else on earth. I smile to myself as I pull out my note-pad and pen and start scribbling down ideas for the next book I want to do, deciding that it has to be about her, one last look at her to kill her off for good. I pretend not to mind that she didn't tell me her story, as she promised she would. But I do mind. It makes me restless and dissatisfied. So I close my eyes, tormenting myself with an image of her beneath me, wild with abandon like an unleashed animal, drowned in pleasure.

When I hear her say 'I'm sorry. Do you mind? That's my seat. Over by the window,' it takes all the strength I possess not to leap to my feet and rip her to shreds with kisses, the urge to beat her and caress her too great to trust myself with, both of them cancelling one another out so that in fact all I do is sit tight for a second, then open my eyes to take a look at her, the inevitability of her blank gaze.

I stand up to let her through, avoiding catching her eye or touching her just yet. 'I was lost. These trains are never-ending,' she says with a grimace and faint little laugh which sounds more like the edge of a sob. 'I had to go through about six carriages. I could've been walking until Christmas! Thank God I found you in the end.'

X

Once more, the two of us are side by side, sliding forwards into the afternoon. She says nothing as she settles herself into the seat beside me. She even turns to look out of the window at the streaming tracks, sighing contentedly, as though everything were perfectly normal. I watch her in amazement, thinking *Is that it? No explanation? No accusations? And where was she all last night? Maybe she is the guilty one? Maybe I was right? Certainly, she can't have been back to the hotel – she has no luggage. Yet now she's here again, pretending nothing's happened. Doesn't she know I meant to get rid of her?* My mind is gritting its teeth with aggravation, not knowing the best way to deal with the situation at all but anyway turning to her and saying 'Well?' with a meaningful look: *can't you see, I didn't want you here?*

And what does she do? She damn well smiles at me. But it's a smile which doesn't even begin to register in her eyes, and I know what that means. She can't believe that I'd ever do what I did last night. She looks at me expectantly, slightly confused, waiting for me to continue. I'm dumbstruck. The things I need to tell her, too many things even to begin, with her sitting there beside me, baffled by the violent expression which is no doubt plastered across my face at this moment.

I tell myself: stay calm. They told me I'd have to treat her gently, 'Take good care of her,' they said. 'Don't expose her to stress of any kind. Be patient. Make her feel secure.' All these things which are a million miles from what I have done and how I now feel, which is brutal, impotent, anguished, despairing, volatile. Likely, in fact, to do anything but what they told me I'd have to do, to help her through. She's waiting for me to go on, watching my lips with great concentration as though she has all the time in the world. I don't know where to start. I want to pin her down and shine a light in her face bellowing *Why?* at her until she gives me some kind of explanation. Explanation of anything that can help me wade out of this impulse to brutalise her, because right now all I can see is that one red thought. It bruises my mind, goading me on to make demands of her.

'Is it me?' she says quietly, her voice almost a whisper. 'Is it something I've done?' And she means this with all her heart. She thinks she's to blame, God help her, so what can I do? 'Of course not. No, there's nothing wrong,' I tell her, smiling like a whore, my shabby anger groaning with the weight of itself, crashing to the bottom of my guts until next time. 'Look,' she says, rummaging in her bag, 'I had this.'

She shows me the piece of paper they gave her at the hospital, with the station names and train times on it. She reaches over towards me and presses the scrap of paper into my hands. 'But were you going to go without me?' she asks, her lips trembling as though she might cry. 'No, no,' I insist, lying through my teeth, 'I knew you'd make it, kiddo. I could never leave without you, you know that.' She looks into my face as though she expects that I'll laugh at any moment, making fun of her. It's unbearable. I pull her towards me and she's unresisting.

'I searched all night. But I couldn't find you,' she says, her voice reaching me from the bottom of a well, a watery, mournful sound. 'It was a nightmare. I looked for you everywhere.'

I cup her head in my hand, feeling the too-fragile weight of her skull with its foul covering of shorn hair. She leans closer towards me and I can sense the vibrations of terror shivering along her veins. Her skull's soft throb is beneath my fingertips. I can look at her clenching, unclenching hands, worrying themselves into motion and I know my mistake. She said that she looked everywhere for me. I now know where she found me: gliding unharmed through the afternoon with my pen uselessly marking the pages of a notebook. She sees me. The sight troubles her because she recognises its origins and, first-hand, feels its conclusions. But do I see her? Do I?

'I'm here with you now,' I tell her, stroking her damp face, not knowing what the hell those words mean. Who is here for who? The very thought of *her being anywhere* fills me with despair. It seems absurdly implausible. I can tell she suspects this now, and only too well, seeing herself caricatured in that ludicrous note still held in my fist. Where she should be, and when, become the only thing she can cling to, no mystery of control, no pretence of hiding inside another more-real life when she feels like it.

So this is how we pass the time on the train journey: trying our hardest to forget everything but the present moments. Acting out the parts we know will get us to the right destination. It's a pact. It makes me feel hopeful. It has something to do with trust and willing blindness, but beyond that I know nothing.

She asks about the house, whether I have been spending much time there. I tell her not to worry, mentioning the changes that have happened while she's been away, trees cut down, the lake freezing over. There are five stations before ours and I'm terrified she'll do a bunk if she is given half a chance. So I don't let her out of my sight. I even follow her down to the loo with some excuse to get fresh air in the corridor and I think she reads this the way it's intended: we've come too far to be separated again.

The countryside grinds past, dirty land and dirty buildings with apparently no chance of snow to transform things, only the grey covering of frost making the whole scene appear to be hidden behind a theatrical gauze, faintly implausible and scum-covered with pollution. We reach our station around five and already the light is failing fast. I'm glad of the darkness and I'm certain that she is, too. It's not much protection but it's something. Only a few other people get off at this stop, heaving their Christmas shopping along with them, laughing nervously and steaming up the frozen air, so we have to be quick about getting ourselves out on to the platform before the train starts to snake away again down the tracks, the rising hum of metal motion shrouding us in deafened isolation. I help her on with her hat and gloves, wrapping myself around her for a moment. She seems so small and afraid. Her eyes stay fixed on me, not looking at any other thing on the platform, just boring into me as though that's the place she'll discover where she is.

I hold her still, tight against myself. 'You're going to be OK,' I tell her over and over as though by telling her I can make it a fact. 'We'll be at the house soon, and it's Christmas Eve, there's nothing to worry about now, everything will be fine.'

Over her head I see a man with two small children standing at the barrier like a little welcome party, looking out for someone they are to meet off the train. Why now? I hope she does not notice them. Then the children suddenly start scampering down the platform towards us, crashing into their mother like tiny missiles, lifting their arms to be picked up. I can feel her body go tense in my arms, a little exhalation of sorrow as she remembers. It had been cruel, that doctor warning her of the risk of a third miscarriage, the end of hope. 'I couldn't bear it,' she said over and over like an affirmation of secure defeat. Now, as we walk through the station I sneak a look at her. She looks back at me, just one thing in her eyes. Despair. It freezes my blood. I can tell that she sees no way out.

Back at the house, events take over. Tomorrow is Christmas Day. There are things to prepare. So we get busy with this strange distraction. I watch her like a hawk. She plays the part well, but I can tell that that's all she's doing, playing a part, not yet convinced that this is her life. I tell her that she must be tired with all this travelling, which gives her a way out. I take her upstairs to the bedroom, telling her, 'I'll be up soon.'

Now it's around nine and the old house is restful. Outside, the silence is absolute. I'm sitting beside the fire in the kitchen, watching the flames, adjusting to the idea of having her around again, not adjusting really, so much as wondering what it's going to be like. I take a long draught of whisky and listen to the night.

So silently does she come into the room that I barely hear her, though I thought I had been attentive to every sound. 'You didn't come to find me,' she says. An accusation. But without malice. 'There you are,' I say. 'I wanted to let you sleep.' She glides across the room towards me and stands behind my back, putting her arms around my neck, leaning down to kiss the top of my head and in this gesture I can almost feel the swoosh of her once-long hair as it brushes across my cheeks. But now there is nothing and her kiss is enough to fill me up with her again. I reach backwards to pull her closer towards me, feeling the delicate pressure of her fingers against my throat as she wraps herself more tightly about me. Her strength surprises me. It reveals her need. 'Come on,' she says, standing up, 'Come with me.'

We go up the stairs together, her slightly ahead, leading me, smiling at me through the darkness of the corridors. In the bedroom the curtains are open on to the night and there is an almost-full moon gleaming wetly upon us as we fall to the bed. 'I'd no idea,' she says, 'about the forest and everything. I'd forgotten. It's so quiet. Beautiful.' And I remember how she used to hate the silence here. 'It's driving me crazy,' she said the first time, flicking up the volume on the stereo, laughing, saying, 'can't we get a tape of traffic sounds? This is unnatural.' I roll her over so that I'm covering her body completely with mine, looking down at her face which is turned towards the window, her surprised eyes shining with the light from the moon. *I'm the one who has had no idea*, I think to myself. I had no idea that it would end up like this, with me feeling as helpless as this but only wanting to help, knowing there's not much I can do but still wanting to try, just my way of paying tribute to the fire in her, because at last I can see that she's for real, not someone I made up. It sounds simple but it's taken me years of experimentation and mistakes to work it out.

She looks up at me, closing her eyes, pulling my head down towards her, kissing me deeply, her hands pressing their way along my back, fitting me to her again as we make love, dissolving into one another for a time.

Afterwards, exhausted, I start to drift to sleep, holding her tight against me, still not quite believing how things have turned out, my mind subdued, off its guard, trying not to ask *Is this the end? This is how we'll be together from now on? So I'll write a happy story?* knowing I've tried it before and look what happened, only monsters.

But that life has ended for me, I say to myself. Everything has changed. Now I need to be self-sufficient, not living like some hideous vampire, sucking sustenance from everyone I set eyes on. I try to tell myself that this thought does not fill me with dread. But I know how hard it will be, and I don't know that I have that degree of self-control, nor the reserves of invention to let me breathe under water for long enough.

I watch the moon. Her body is curved against my chest to fit, her toes curled up against my shins. She is lying dead still, her breathing an even rhythm which fills me with anxiety, making my own breath become shallow with simulation: I am happy, I tell myself, things have worked out better than even I could have imagined. I'm at home with my wife. *Things are settled.* She will get better, eventually, she will. They said they could help her overcome the worst of it and that with time and care she should be fine. This is the perfect ending. What more could I ask for, for God's sake? But against my brain, the heavy thud of anxiety, the gut fear of predictability, days replicating and reproducing themselves, the endless duplication meaning merely death. I try not to shudder with the vision of this soft slide into the earth, hating myself for being restless so soon. I loathe the direction my thoughts are taking, already turning around and heading back to her, scrutinising her in my mind's eye and thinking of the stories fomenting in that hot-wired brain of hers.

I jump, physically scared out of my wits, when as though from out of nowhere, her voice, this time deep and steady, tells me, 'Don't worry, I haven't forgotten that I said I'd give you the whole story.' And I feel the hot rush of excitement, gratitude, too, at her telepathic sleeplessness. 'You want to know everything?' she asks, wriggling around to face me, her eyes serious with concentration. I try not to show too much eagerness, knowing it must be written all over my greedy face.

'Yes,' I tell her, making the third big mistake of my life. The first was meeting her, the second, doubting her, the third, sincerely wanting to know her, despite my better judgment. 'Yes,' I say, smiling like a sick dog, 'please, tell me everything.'

Two

I

Yes, well, here it goes again, Mia tells herself, watching him walk towards her through the crowded street. *Here I am, blessed again*, she thinks, wishing it were otherwise. Blessings aren't free. They come heavily burdened. So already Mia is wondering how long it will be until she can be rid of him.

'Could you tell me how I get to Haymarket from here? I want to walk,' she asks, reeling him in with a look of innocence.

And he is brought up short like a wounded bird shot down with perfect accuracy, suddenly dead still in the middle of the writhing air, eddying in brisk motion around them as they make an island of themselves, people flooding by on either side.

His eyes widen slightly as though in disbelief. They have a dead, wolverine pallor that reminds her of sharpened metal in moonlight. Then the colour heightens in his cheeks, only a slight alteration but it tells her enough. He takes a pace closer towards her, arms twitching at his sides as though wanting to loop her in an embrace. His lips appear to tremble. She recognises the signs. Both of them are on the alert, like partnered divers swallowing air before slipping beneath the skin of the sea.

That morning she woke with the birds. Screaming outside her window they reminded her of something she had forgotten:

a child's game she used to play by herself on the first day of spring. Dressing as if for an exploration, she would spend the entire day walking the warm fields which smelt of new grass not yet grown but pressing its tips above the skin of the earth as she walked upon it, feeling heroic. This is what Mia remembered that morning.

The dawn was still a slow fade into colour unbearably delicate on the horizon. Few car sounds meant secrecy: *I am seeing this alone* she told herself, leaning out of the window to feel the air pressed against the naked surfaces of her skin, wondering, if she went out, would there be others similarly strolling, thinking they were celebrating the first day of spring alone? So she went out into the day to look and there were people in the streets who, sure enough, were walking, but the sightless walk of people already dead, accepting death like a drink of milk in the dark, not even seeing how brightly it shines.

It is as she is walking – and by now she looks raggedy, at least dusty, because she has been walking since dawn – that she first sees Sam. The river is nearby. She can hear it groaning close beside her, though perhaps that is the traffic. In her mind's eye Mia sees the river stretched out through the city, curving its way through it like a temptress, sinuous and strong, the glassy buildings along its banks like a thousand sordid hands to be made pure by the endless flood of black water, darkly impenetrable. Despite the hands and the long reflective eyes upon her body, there is always the flood to purify, in the end.

Mia is jealous of this regeneration, for she feels time's passage like a fast ebb of arterial blood. For her, life holds only

memory's short stabs of concreted desires, unlinked by anything but a longing for possession. *I am sliding life by*, she often
thinks to herself after each unanchored yearning dissolves, but
remains remembered, silted up in the dark parts of her mind.

Just before she sees him, Mia stands on the brink, listening to
the guttural outbreathing river. She can feel the imprint of his
eyes upon her the way one feels a change in the light: with the
precision of unfettered senses. She feels, too, that when she
turns her head the whole scene shudders slightly, trembling on
the edge of chaos, as though her head-turning is of equal
significance to the sound of the grey sand shifting along the
guts of the riverbed, or that her eye fixed momentarily upon a
southwesterly-bound bird matters as much as her right hand's
death-grip upon whoever might chance against the inquisitive
dance of fingers on flesh.

Mia would soon realise that it made perfect sense to see Sam
when she did, at the centre of this fragile scene. All around the
edges of her flesh, the cool first day of spring is barely warmed
by the low sun. Reflected off the river, the light gives their two
figures an insubstantial, almost underwater appearance. For
Mia, it is a moment of uncalm sensation, hot-burning with
sadness and suddenly quiet, too, a vision of *how things are*
compressed into one brief breath of time.

'So what happens when you get to Haymarket?' he asks her
above the din of the river, the traffic, the bawling people, the
spring air buzzing in her eardrums as it tickles its way down her
back to the root of her spine. Mia tells him that she might be
meeting someone there later to see a film. She watches the way
he leans slightly towards her when he speaks, as though

similarly deafened by the noises all around them. She loves the island they have made. It feels like a promise and when he lowers his dark head closer towards hers, she can smell the cool breath of his skin, newly washed and wet-smelling like the fresh edge of a winter lake. He touches his hair to move away a black strand that has fallen across his forehead. He appears to do it without thinking, and she wonders what else he does that is purely involuntary, noticing the way he breathes, shallow breaths but quiet as though after a lofty run downhill, measuring the speeding pace with a song.

Sam's hands are soft-palmed, huge and strong-fingered like a sculptor's or strangler's, clever at working without sight, with the svelte darkness wrapped tight around him as he wrestles with his secret pleasure, unseen. To talk to her, he has to curve the span of his shoulders downwards slightly, the movement making her feel almost embraced and the *almost* being in fact a confident expectation: she knows they will see more of each other than this.

'You can't go to the cinema,' he says. 'Not on a beautiful day like this. There may not be another like it for ages.' So they go to a place he describes, with a garden where they can sit outside in the sunlight. He says, 'Take my arm,' with an almost mocking incline of his head, appearing too certain of himself as he leads her through the traffic. 'It's better to walk along the river bank don't you think? It isn't far,' he says. And she finds it sweet as can be to relinquish responsibility to someone as charming and determined as he is, swooping along with her so she almost has to leap to keep up.

They cross to the other side of the road, at last slowing down to find a matching rhythm of legs and arms swinging along together beside the river. Mia is aware of everything that is going on around her only as it affects the consummation of the hungry pact she knows they have silently set up: to see where this will take them.

His arm through hers is warm and strong. He holds on tight. She can feel the soft cotton of his shirt rubbing against the bare skin of her elbow and with her other hand, surreptitiously, she touches the bright blue fabric to see how it feels beneath her fingertips. But he notices the touch and turns slightly towards her, smiling. His eyes are smiling, too, and his lips close as he breathes a fast, unheard out-breath through his nostrils, swallowing, his eyes fixed on hers at first, then slipping down towards her lips and staying there, too long. Mia looks away and points towards the river, describing something to Sam that makes him laugh, the threads of complicity binding them tighter.

She can see the eagerness in his eyes, the certainty rising up like a declaration, telling her his conviction: *this chance encounter has all the makings of a happy story.* She can tell that he is thinking this, also that the thought has surprised him, a vision of her naked nocturnal body darting like a pretty fish into his mind, perhaps, as he contemplates the smooth curve of her face, turned from him.

They walk closer to the edge. By jumping up on to the parapet which runs along the river bank, she can see the fast surface twitch darkly in the sunlight. She is taller than him this way and when, laughing, he says 'Careful!' as she slips, there is a look of surprise on his face. But she can see that it is surprise at himself, not her. He is not worried that she might fall, only worried that this would bother him, so unused to being bothered. It fills her with an urge to leap empty-handed into the river to see what he would do. She is grateful for his anxious look, though resentful, too: it carries an obligation with it.

Above them now, cherry blossoms and pale horse-chestnut buds tremble in the light wind and she is sure there will be rain, any moment. She thinks she can hear it running softly along the surface of the wide water. But it's a fast spring shower that barely darkens the sky and their even pace is unbroken as the rain hurtles earthwards, making the dust rise in the road and the river fizz as raindrops tickle its skin with unseen spikes of mysterious silver.

Smiling, they turn their faces up towards the rain as though it were sunshine, secretly knowing that had they been alone they might have stopped for a moment, waiting beneath the shelter of a tree until it passed. Only, now, together, they are finding it delicious, their sight softened with the underwater secrecy of walking beside a whole river of raindrops: the pleasure in ordinary things done freely.

The shower is soon over, hotly chased by sun. They shake their heads like dogs, scattering raindrops. 'It's not far now,' he says as they stand still for a moment, looking up at the cloudless sky. Then more quietly, 'Just a little further.' His face seems suddenly puzzled as he reaches towards her forehead to move aside a piece of pale hair that has fallen into her eyes. But his expression reveals his fear, and he touches her as though he expects her to dissolve. He lowers his hand quickly then, and looks down at the pavement, turning as if to go but touching her again, lightly, on the shoulder, to guide her in the right direction. She takes hold of his arm. He looks ahead, and she can see that he is grinning, his shoulders pressed back with happiness.

This is how they walk, arms linked, smiling, strolling along the river bank and on into the bright afternoon.

II

S am is standing, framed in the doorway, looking out at her from the darkness. 'Will you come inside?' he asks, 'or do you want to get a place over there in the sunshine?' He seems to fill the doorway, blocking out the light.

'I'll be over there,' Mia tells him, pointing, going over to sit on the wall beneath the apple tree in the far corner of the garden.

When she glances back at him he is still standing there, watching her, though even turned from him her back burns with the thought of his eyes upon it. She wonders what he sees when he looks at her. When she turns back towards the door again, he has gone inside. She stares at the murky emptiness which has dissolved him and feels a rush of disappointment, wishing she didn't. She thinks about running away now, before this goes any further. But just to think this makes her panic, wondering if he is having the same thoughts. Perhaps even now he has sneaked out by the side entrance of the bar?

She waits for him. Without wishing it, a future vision of herself, similarly lying in wait for him, flashes into her mind. Waiting is not a form of passivity, she realises, but a willing hibernation of desire and aggression. To be able to wait, in a position of calm contentment, without this quickening, restless dissatisfaction, that would be a kind of wisdom. But she cannot do it. She waits and she starts to hate, brooding with the certainty that her hatred is merely the first inkling of wanting something that she can never fully possess: his fixed desire, given without demands for revenue.

Mia looks over towards the doorway at the exact moment that Sam appears in it, carrying drinks. He is there suddenly, as though leaping out from the darkness into the light, looking for her. When he sees her, his face brightens with an expression that is part relief, part fear: it's not over yet. 'I thought you might have done a bunk,' he says. 'But I'm glad you didn't. Isn't this pleasant?' he adds, smiling, handing her a large whisky.

So they sit there beside one another on the wall, their legs dangling over the edge and bumping together like bobbing floats at sea. She asks him to tell her about himself. He tells her the facts of his life. She finds it reassuring, the way he is prepared to tell her only brute details, his name, that he's a writer, when and where he was born, what he does when he's not working, where he lives, where he has travelled to. *These facts could belong to anyone*, she thinks, glad of this chance of anonymity. It makes her feel light. She is grateful to him for not burdening her with the weight of his disappointments and hopes, especially since she can tell how deeply he feels these two things: disappointment, hope. She sees them in his eyes when he looks into hers. His eyes ask *how soon?* She knows he wants something from her and is unsurprised when he starts to turn all her questions around. She sees his vampire's teeth and can hear the warnings he is casting out towards her. False life-lines. 'So tell me, after that what happened?' he asks, discreetly hungry, 'and how did that make you feel?'

Yet Mia takes his attentiveness to be a form of flattery. She thinks it means that he is merely curious to know her. So she tries to give him everything. Besides, she badly wants rid of it. Her life weighs too heavily upon her. She feels herself to be no more than the sum of her actions, so that everything she has ever done amounts to everything that she is – no more nor less than that. *Soon, but not yet, my life will start*, she tells herself, longing for a love so great that she could abandon everything to it. She wants to cast off the heaviness of having lived as she has, afloat on a sea of isolation. And in that way, Mia thinks, she could be free.

But that their meeting should be of less significance than if he had cut his hand on a rose thorn, watching the blood-drop drip and the tiny scar gently suppurate and then heal – this thought horrifies her. She wants to make her mark upon him. She thinks: *I want to stop him dead in his tracks and give him everything that I am*, just so that she can be released for a moment from the voracious oppressions of time. She looks time in the eye and it appears to her to be like a dark tunnel, so dark that she cannot even see herself in it.

Mia closes her eyes, trying not to imagine the earth's hot, blood-burning speed, the endless spin into emptiness. She wants to be able to keep her eyes tight shut to the maggoty future, always lurking beneath the fragrant, cool crust of the land. But she cannot do this. She is rabbited in the glare of perpetual motion. When she opens her eyes, no more than a second later, Sam is watching her lips, waiting for her to tell him something else but she tells him nothing. She has given up on words. He can tell she has, too. She can see it in his eyes. The little fear starting up in his brain like flames.

'Look,' he says, lightly touching her wrist with his fingertips, pointing behind her so that she has to move closer towards him as she turns to look at the cooling sun, low in the sky, darkening to a deep orange, making the river appear to burn as it melts its way through the city. His eyes are on fire, too, but they hold no warmth and she can tell that his hunger is rooting around in his guts, goading him on, making him want her without any reason beyond hunger.

She can see that he hates this, his flesh's cry for satisfaction, that he doesn't know what it means. He suspects it means nothing. But he wishes that it meant something beyond this subtle, sinuous aching, nudging at his blood so that all he can do is follow where his flesh takes him, which is towards her. This time, it's towards her.

'Your hair is on fire,' he says, laughing, his fingertips dancing towards her, waiting. 'Yours too,' she tells him, stroking his dark hair which does not burn – she lied – it absorbs the light as though unaffected by brightness. He smiles a smile of relief and she feels the blood in her veins start to shiver faster, waking up from the inhuman, death-loving day into this chance of night, the sun sinking now into the water behind them, fading silently as its fire is put out.

'Are you cold?' he wants to know, taking her hands in his and lifting them to his lips to make sure of their size and taste in his mouth. Between fingertips twining, tight-pressed skin, eyes closing out the rest of sight to see only the one chosen other, there is nothing. And with the whole world shut out from these nascent dimensions of pleasure, the fine line between bodies, once breached, creates a vital illusion. *Being just flesh* becomes implausible then, always seeming, falsely, to reveal something beyond itself.

Now the sun is entirely hidden beneath the rim of the land and the embered city begins to burn with a cooler light. Birds swing from their windy perches high up in the treetops and early bats wheel and shudder above the bridge, with the boiling river dark-boiling beneath, as they cross over towards the unseen alleyways on the other side.

Through all of this, they are wrapped up together, seldom losing touch – always the magnetised return to sweat-close proximity. She longs to cut out all other sound and hear only their two drums of blood beating into one another. But the loud pound booms hotly so that she shakes with it, her limbs become traitors, demanding release.

They reach the doorway to her house. Pressed against it, she can feel his weight like a gift as he leans into her, covering her with his hot hands. The only thought she has: *more*. She imagines herself as a feasting clock, with its fang-dripping tick-tock to mark the minutes before *more* becomes *enough* and then straightaway *more* until the whole thing flows like molten rocks, its speed and heat become incredible. His hands are huge. When he puts them on her body she feels touched to her guts. It's as though his hands are spades, digging with hungry precision just the right amount of tenderness to make her almost weep with it.

'You're going to kill me!' she hears him say, the words breathed out tight against her neck, making her pull back suddenly. He raises his head to look at her. She smiles, clawing his naked throat in pretence of violence. His panic is dissolved by desire. He takes a tighter hold of her, careless of his own vulnerability.

She watches his hands through the darkness, seeing his fingers race across her skin like mad animals, weirdly exotic. His dark eyes swallow her sight until she looks away and then they are falling backwards, staggering like drunks into the house. The door closes behind him as he pulls her closer, shutting out the night.

III

The smooth marble is like ice against her back as she stretches out in the hallway. Mia feels the cold stone through the fabric of her dress as he bends her bones against the floor. There is a red and blue light dappling their bodies, cast through the windowpanes from the street outside. When he raises his head the scarlet light is painted right across his face making him look like a devil with black eyes, red teeth. She turns away.

He smiles down at her, touching her hair. 'Like this,' he says, 'You look like an angel.'

It is this pressing on into night that she lives for. She feels certain that she will soon be free of him. This thought makes her glad and already she senses the thrill of liberation. She hopes that he will take something of her away with him, and in this way leave her lighter than before. She watches him eating up each part of her as his eyes fall upon it, washing her with the wet reflection of his desire.

His hands pull her up hard against him and through the darkness his eyes are glittering, the brightness of the insane shining within them, covering her with black looks and lunatic hunger, eating inspiring appetite not satisfaction, always wanting more. With his hands like this, around her hips, dragging her against him, it feels as though he wants to break her, remake her, throw her aside when he's done and she wants him to understand that she knows this need better than any other: it's the only one that tells the truth, embracing the life-death quick stamp of succession without sentiment.

His head in her hands feels apelike, primitively huge, a brutish, blunt shape, but soft-haired, and the nape of his neck bends backwards when she bites it, tasting the texture of his softly curling black hair against her lips made salty by his sweating skin. He smells of sea-washed flesh and his ears in her mouth make him groan, twitching with pleasure and surprise. Her arms, stretched out to pull him against her, only just reach around his back which she clings to, an impulse sudden as vertigo.

She suspects she has slept for a long time. Her body barely knows what to do. It acts on instincts unfamiliar to her. She watches it from a distance. Its efficiency soon makes her sweat. She feels grateful. She had begun to believe that it had died without ceremony, the carefully stored remembrance of lust no more than memory, contemplated with disbelief and rarely.

But his hands are upon her, and she feels the rush of skin-shock as they divulge new stretches of flesh. He makes her feel like a black pit of sensation, not bound in by legs, ankles, fingers, breasts, a belly, cunt, backbone, none of these, since all of these, once touched, seem dissolved by his hands. She is sure he must be able to hear the voices muttering hot urgency all along the edges of her skin, the pattering murmur of desire which makes her tremble, almost deaf with longing.

His lips are against her ear now. She knows that he is telling her secrets only in the hope that she will not hear them – that she will receive his confession without judgment, mistaking his honesty for craziness when he whispers, 'Now I've found you I'll never let you go.' And this declaration seems important to her, although she doesn't yet know what it will mean.

She presses her fingers, one by one, against the ridges of his spine, imagining the blood and meat inside him, trying to think of him as nothing more than that, feeling the tensing muscles, bunching into pleasure as though trying to burn right through her and blank out all other sensations in her body but him. Her tongue against the side of his neck traces the textures of unknown skin, and laps up the tastes of him before he met her, only a few hours ago. She wants to bite into him to know him better, feel his flesh in her mouth, his blood on her face. She wants his blood to flow with hers in a final river to join them in even one brute fact, something, anything, beyond this sensation soon over.

And that's the worst part of it, Mia thinks as she leads him with sudden tenderness to her bedroom: *this is an ending, not a beginning, and we are already strangers.* It's a lie, his 'I'll never let you go.' He is already letting her go, even by taking a hold of her as he now is, his huge hands upon the buttons of her dress, making clumsy work of undoing the tiny fastenings, his ebony eyes glittering at her through the darkness.

From outside in the street, the infrequent cars slip their headlights across the room, sliding the putrid colour over them like contemplation, deciding what shade they should be, always ending with the blind black night. He is eloquent when he tumbles her bedwards, pulling her clothes softly from her.

Nothing like this: the first time with a new body, the first and last chance of hope contained in flesh.

But with Sam upon her like this – closer now that she has wriggled him out of his jeans, stretched his shirt over his head so that she can lick the wide weight of his chest before she slides further down to bite his hip, feeling the bone just beneath the surface of his skin, then his warm cock, the skin softer than milk against her tongue making her ache for him, wanting him as an animal wants to kill at night, scenting the defeated flesh and drawn to it – like this, and for the entire duration of flesh-pressed proximity, she is freed from herself.

Possessing her, he kills the person she was before, and each new instant, held, becomes obsolete. She is giddy with the lightness of inexistence.

So on into the final nightmoves. She drags him into her like a maniac intent on nothing else but that: to be filled up by him, banishing herself so that she can feel only him, see only who he thinks she is reflected in his famished eyes. She wonders how soon it will be until he's gone. If not gone by his own volition, then tired of by her.

He holds her head in his meatish fists, pinning her down, all his strength pushed into driving hard and harder inside her. She can tell that he is watching her eyes to see where he has got to because, like her, he's terrified that maybe *she's the one*, that maybe his *never leave you* means what he thinks it does, which would be disastrous. It would incur too much change. And suddenly she sees in this coupling the one thing she tries to avoid at all costs: wanting more than the present moment.

But the rub of flesh is all Mia thinks of, deliberately shutting out thoughts of later. He fits inside her as though doing gentle damage, the plunder of hard and soft, each minute patch of skin, touched, enflamed and pushed to the limits of pleasure. Soon she feels his body begin to shudder on the brink of helplessness, not wanting the end but seeing it and knowing it has to be soon. She shuts her eyes, finding relief in darkness, no longer his questioning gaze which horrifies her.

She feels his knuckles burn into her shoulders, almost breaking the skin, his fingers gripping tight like a man on the edge of a cliff, hanging on for dear life as he pounds out his last drop of strength. She grips his back, dragging him further down into the deep sea of painpleasure with her, trembling as though on fire with a stream of wild water flooding through her, unbearably quiet at first with every inch of her locked into a silent orbit against the logic of human flesh as though synapse-struck with a slice of steel, so that the sum total of what she is is this isolated moment of sensation, lifted above the waves of time.

Transformed by this instant of delirium, she is released from herself. This is what Mia most wants from life – were it not for the extreme solitude, utterly impossible to be reconciled to the everyday hum of living.

They peel apart from one another and slip back into time so that she starts to notice things again: traffic in the street outside, his breathing, stertorous and strong, the slipping lights sliding across the ceiling, transfiguring the space around them, making his body appear marmoreal and suddenly serene. She doubts that she should touch it but when she does he turns to her straightaway and folds her up in his arms, pulling her closer towards him, pressing her face against his chest as he kisses the top of her head. She feels young and bereft, all things new, asking herself *What will I do now, without him?*

'You can leave now if you like because this is enough,' Mia tells him, muttering against his chest, 'I don't need more.' Sam saying 'Leave? I'll never leave you. How could I? I'm going to make you mine.' And his fingers find out the secret places along the valleys of her body, around her throat and wrists, holding her so tightly that she feels weightless, crushed by him.

Soon it will be morning. She squeezes closer against him, listening to the words he is weaving around her like jewelled promises, although he promises nothing. When he sleeps his breathing finds a pattern and she slips inside that secret music, tiny inhalations like a child's they seem so shallow. And throughout all of this, his nocturnal sweetness, she feels his hands tightly gripped about her like a drowning man clinging to the last rock he can find, though already far beneath the surface of the hopeless water.

This is how they spend many nights, that first spring and beyond, sliding into the darkness with him clinging to her, oblivious to how contented his face looks in sleep. And it is his embrace – even in sleep – that matters most to her. It seems to be a sign somehow of the unfathomable prevalence of flesh, acting out its delicate intentions without the slowing drudge of the everyday, making two bodies wrapped up together something far more precious than words or the repetitions of daylight.

IV

One day, Mia wakes to find Sam watching her. His face is black. The light is behind him. He sits turned away from the window which boxes him in from behind so that he appears trapped, framed by the white space.

The moment she wakes, he gets up and comes to sit beside her on the bed, leaning down towards her to place a kiss on her forehead which is still warm with sleep. The night behind them is bright in her memory and when he lifts her out from beneath the bedclothes, reaching right around to gather her up tightly in his arms, she feels the heat of his body like a reminder of solitude: Mia's pleasure in his flesh bursts vividly into her mind's eye so that she actually shakes with the thought of him inside her – an incommunicable sensation. She wonders if he knows yet what he has started.

He holds her hard against him and when she pulls back to look at his face he is smiling, a warm smile of disbelief. 'I don't deserve this much luck,' he says, grinning broadly. 'It's not luck,' she tells him, curious why he describes it like that. 'I might turn out to be a monster, and then what?' He laughs when she says this, tipping his head back as though this were the funniest thing he ever heard. She presses against his chest, hoping he doesn't see the panic edging its way across her face as she feels the slip from who she is into who he imagines she might be.

'Darling girl,' he says to her, 'you are so sweet.' He kisses her hair and lifts her up higher so that he can kiss her face. Her lips and his are all that she wants for now, his lips against her skin, wherever against her flesh he chooses to press them. 'You don't know me at all,' she says, truthfully. 'I know all I need to, for now,' he says. And she wonders how it is possible for someone to be so fearless. Isn't it obvious? Doesn't he see yet what will happen? But that will come later *and now* she says to herself, *his lips and body, nothing else.*

So that is all there is for a time, closing out the rest of the world again as they tussle and tremble their wet way to satisfaction. For the duration of struggle, all thoughts of continuation are rooted to the just-beyond-present moments. And even when daylight floods the room, laying bare their bodies to sullen scrutiny, still, her desire for him remains.

It is not usually like this for Mia. She loses interest quickly. Happiness frustrates her. She detests what it does to two people feeling it simultaneously. Like religion, it promises an afterlife it cannot deliver. It makes believe that there is some purpose to things, when there is none.

So when Sam turns to her, saying, 'I'm happy here like this, aren't you?' she can hear the edge of horror cutting through his voice like ice, even if he doesn't hear it yet himself, and she wonders how soon it will be before his happiness starts to disgust him. Because she knows that it will. Sooner than he thinks, he will feel oppressed by it. Then he will realise that the echo of his 'I'm so happy' admission is merely the need for more. He will hate this neediness in himself even more than she already hates it in herself. And then what? What will it make him do? His indirect craving for permanence will surely make him long for escape.

He leans towards her, lying on his side, propping himself up on one arm so that he can take a better look at her. They lie facing one another, trying to work out the ending. He reaches out his fingertips to press tiny patterns along her neck and shoulders, then across her hips, stroking her as he might stroke a cat, a smooth, considered touch as though anticipating surprises. It is clear that he suspects she might leap up and run away, given half a chance. And it's true, this is exactly what she had been intending to do, before dawn.

But Mia was foolish. She let herself sleep. Even as she slept, she knew that this was what she was doing. Her hunger kept her there, a compliant captive, remaining in his house. And now this regular stretching stroke soft across her skin is something unexpected. She feels calmed by it. It's as though his tentative discovery of the shape of her is in fact remaking her into the shape he imagines, at this early stage, that she fits into. He is like a man testing the waters of a tiny ocean with his bleeding toes, not yet noticing the red ooze as it floods through the blue. She watches him to see what it is he sees. She waits for clues.

Beyond the window the sun is already bright-shining and the warm rays, beaming in through the open window, heat up the bare skin of her back. 'It's a beautiful day,' she says, stretching in the sunlight, 'let's go out.'

Sam grins, taking Mia's hand to pull her up from the bed and lead her through to the bathroom. He never takes his eyes from her. He is fixing her, naming things about her, describing things to himself so that he can retell them later and in that way find them easier to forget. Naming things absolves people from their otherwise spiral into sensuality. Easier to forget things that fit into catalogues, the weird regiment of inhuman systems.

He watches her as she steps into the water, sinking beneath the surface, submerged. She can feel him sitting beside the bath, waiting for her to come up for air. She can see him there even with her eyes shut, sensing the shape of him – a dark silhouette of watchfulness like a jungle cat made keen with waiting. She feels her lungs' swollen alarm as she stays beneath the water, and when she breaks the surface, there he is as she knew he would be, thinking he's getting to know her, deciding what kind of a woman he thinks she is, of what type. He clearly imagines that he knows women. He dismisses them by reducing them to an articulate description. *Well then, that's how I will escape him*, Mia tells herself as she washes, feeling his black eyes upon her like a judgment.

When the telephone rings in the bedroom next door, he answers it with irritation that turns to affection, then evasion. She knows it is another woman. She can imagine perfectly well the lies he has told her, the dance away from commitment he is making in his, 'No, I'm busy. Honey, look, can I call you later?' And when he comes back through to the bathroom, he tells her, 'People always want something from me. You'd be surprised. Maybe I'm too generous. They always want more.'

There is no trace of irony in Sam's voice when he tells her this, nor in Mia's when she says, 'You poor thing. You must learn to say no.' But it is clear that she is mocking him, although he would call it flirtation. She steps out of the bath, turning from him. She doesn't want him to see the disappointment she feels at his petulant warning – 'They always want more' – because she also understands his threat to be a challenge.

It is early afternoon when they leave the house. The streets are humming. They go into the park, walking beneath the shade of ash trees with their leaves furled like buds. They can hear the sap drip in the silences between footsteps, their soft pad across the earth, cracking the grass with extreme delicacy as though on stilts. His hand holds hers within it. His fingers are cool, they touch her skin with definite deliberation, not casually, and all around them there is birdsong and distant traffic, the delicate pattern of late spring in the city. Coming out into the sunlight, the heat hits them in the face like hot silk.

In her mind's eye, they are perfectly human. No more than two humans walking the earth together, bound emphatically on to the same raft, racing smooth and calm above the wild water of living, buoyant and content. There is nothing whatsoever that could complete this picture of how they are right now. It is enough. Every part of her body is vibrating with the clear contentment of it, undistracted. Everything seems simple, everything possible.

They walk up to the brow of the hill. Beneath them, the city, softened by heat-dazed fumes, appears miraculous and somehow remote from the blazing blue sky beaming overhead with bright sunlight and the glint of aeroplanes. On the air: only the sound of the nearby roads and birds singing among the shivering trees, trembling in the slight wind sidling its way up from off the top of the city, along the river to the hilltop where they stand and watch, and nowhere is the sound of any human voice except their own. They lie down flat on the new grass and look at the sky, their hands and feet touching, him sighing like a deep-sea fish might exhale air, languidly, saying, 'This is grand, isn't it?' adding, as though as an afterthought, 'I don't deserve to be this happy, this content. I have no right.'

She knows then, listening to him as he spools out those words for her to catch up, that they don't stand a chance. That up here on the hilltop, overlooking the wreckage of their past lives like this, the city become some magnificent memento, more remembered than seen, that surveying all of this is an act of prayer like burning incense at a shrine. They are not in fact declaring their best intentions, as she had almost begun to hope they might be doing. They are rather tasting the stick of sealing wax as it dries on the pact of their mutual inability to believe that such things as this are possible. They are declaring their uncourageousness, but worse than that: they lack the imagination. Neither of them really believes the fantastical nightdance of words and skin can add up to anything stretched out through time, a tender spinning of bright intention and patience which could be extraordinary.

'It shouldn't be possible, I know,' Mia tells him, 'To be this happy.'

'Perhaps we've made it up,' he says, laughing.

'No, this is real enough,' she replies, for a second in deadly earnest, throwing him a tiny line of hope. He stares her hard in the eye, as though to check that this is true; he sees that it is.

'But how can it last? I'll have to make you mine,' he tells her, feigning playfulness to hide his fear. He looks away, and his defeat is almost tangible: the facts of Sam's life, his character before he met her, have just now caught up with him.

So the afternoon leans deeply into dusk and soon the sun is entirely hidden beneath the furthest edge of the land. The city cools beneath them. She can feel the chill even from up here. It matches his icy fingertips, reminding her warm skin of his resolute separation. She should have guessed how their story would go. Only, realising that she is in love with him, she had started to feel such intense contentment, the kind that makes a mockery of words: they cannot attach themselves to it, it moves too swiftly, a silent animal in the night, seldom seen.

They stroll together down the hillside and back into the labyrinth of streets become threatening. She can see the end approaching in dark corners and behind the warning glare of traffic-lights, through the nightmare gratings above cold-rushing sewers, along the dirty kerbstones, beneath people's shoes as they walk, their feet an aimless threat. And it is at this point, descending into the shadowy end of day, that she notices his expression. His dark eyes, hunted, scan the pavements with restless attention. Mia can feel him flinch each time another man passes them. Sam's tightening grip around her arm signals an absurd accusation. 'See,' he says bitterly, 'you would never be able to give any of *this* up.' But she has done nothing and his jealousy is a fantasy of denial – for which she forgives him. She imagines that it means he is claiming her for himself with only the best intentions.

Still he does not look at her, even when he mutters, too fast for truth, 'I've just remembered. I have to go out later. I promised someone. I probably won't be gone long. You'll be OK?' But he does not look at her for an answer and draws her sharply into step beside him, pulling her closer, winding his arm noose-like about her neck, never breaking step as they walk together through the streets and on into the evening.

V

Sam's sudden disappearances soon become an unexplained part of their life together. They settle into the far corners of Mia's mind, a ceaseless repetition of disbelief, and she feels as though her heart is being silted up with longing – the keen desire for things to be other than as they appear to be. He never tells her where he goes to. She does not like to be persistent.

On one particular night, before Sam leaves, he stands for a moment in the centre of the room, shifting his weight uneasily from foot to foot, pressing his hands into his pockets as though afraid of what he might do with them, were he to let them loose. 'You'll be OK?' he asks, a brief pang of remorse making him falter, slightly, as he heads for the door.

She listens to him thump down the stairs, go outside, the relieved slam of his feet as he walks away fast down the street. He is obviously late.

The evening darkens into night, dusky shadows lengthening across the room. Flicking on the lights through the house, Mia feels the disquiet of someone misplaced. *I should leave now*, she tells herself. She should end this without fuss. But she stays, listening for his return. She can think of nothing but the sensation of waiting. She digests the fury she feels at his absence, swallowing it back with a placebo of pride, hating the taste. Beside her, the alarm clock passes ten, eleven, midnight, with a discreet snapping of internal mechanisms.

At half past midnight, Sam returns, humming quietly. He is fragrant with recent washing, his hair still damp. So obvious is it that he has just fucked another woman, that Mia braces herself for his admission of guilt. But he says nothing, although now he is able to look her squarely in the eye. 'Sorry. I'm later than I thought I'd be.'

He undresses without guile and stands for a moment, naked, in front of her, almost as though for inspection. As he turns slightly, slipping into bed beside her, Mia can see a thin red scratch, new with blood, etched across his left shoulder. A short mark of passionate ownership, not her own. He lies for a moment on his side, looking hard at her face as though she were the one who had something to tell him, before clasping his arms about her, dragging her deeply into his embrace.

Now she lies facing the cool rectangle of window, white-covered to filter out the darkness. She has her back to him but he clings to her from behind, his arms tightly wound about her. She watches the night, the slow fade into dawn. She hears the city emptying itself of noise.

There are hours, sometimes, in the nights here, when there is almost no sound at all and she has to strain hard to hear anything, knowing there will be some noise, somewhere, maybe lurking beyond the edge of hearing, but *there* none the less. Even if it's only the birds falling to earth in their secret funerals, the delicate feathered descent, unnoticed, like a drowned body's slow bloat into blue.

Mia feels the twist of despair inside her as she sinks further into wakefulness, wishing she could sleep the way one wishes for heat. She remembers other mornings, before Sam, walking the dawn to shed the smell of men from her skin, feeling them dissolve from her, wishing they could be something more than smell. She wanted to feel the two-halved union of flesh amount to something beyond itself. It never did. She always left feeling freer than she had before she met them. Their touches left no fingerprints upon her. They anointed her with isolation. She felt solitude start to shine around her even as they pulled her closer against them, wanting to mark her with themselves. *I have become so good at being elusive* she would think, smiling, *that one of these days I won't even be able to find myself.* But she always had to have a way out.

And now? she asks herself. What is my way out now? He denies everything. Her desire to believe him is based on faith alone. But it is not faith in his honesty, rather, a grim faith in the alternative reality he has offered her: he is innocent, she is the guilty one – and he forgives her. So how then could she leave him? What would be her excuse? He has allowed her no options, and all her certainties about what is real, what invention, are cast adrift on a lowering tide of perpetual fictions. She sinks her head as though beneath waves, feeling the bleak pressure on her shoulders, cowing her.

It is at this point that he always lifts her up, holds her fiercely to him, 'You know how I love you,' some new shard of tenderness for her to cut her spirit on, unnoticed wound to her heart, again.

Against the white wall, the shape of Sam's back is solid,

calmly listing like the sea at night. It makes everything else appear insubstantial.

Mia wonders how he sleeps when he is alone. She imagines it is precisely how he is sleeping now, turned that way, his left arm wrapped right around his shoulder and neck as though in an embrace. She suspects he is a lonely man, seldom in fact alone, but hating his craving for solitude which turns into a curse: he needs to feel it, above all. It is his way of being autonomous and untrembled by the wishfulness of others, especially people he cares for. She leans closer towards him to hear him breathing. She loves this sound. His secret life's gentle rhythm which carries on, listened to or not. It reassures her because it is the truth about how things are which otherwise she cannot comprehend: the soft continuation of life in sleep, unperceived yet still persisting.

Mia shuts her eyes. *But he has ruined sleep for me,* she tells herself, wondering if this is what it would feel like to hate him.

On the ceiling, there is a slender crack running the length of the room, spidery, irresolute, broken in numerous places. It ends at the point where ceiling and wall meet: an abrupt cadence of staggering fragility, a hair-thin crack breaking through the otherwise incessant white. Mia imagines herself tracing the path of a skater on a lake at night, underestimating the extent of damage done by the delicate blade of steel as it cuts a fatal flaw.

It's a fine and fragile line across the blankness that Mia is treading. A tenuous slide through nothingness. But it is all she has: she feels that she is nowhere else but in these isolated instants between the frozen weight of time. Only her flesh, disgustingly, drags itself forward. And it perpetuates no more than a vague resemblance to itself, decaying each moment into unfamiliarity.

She listens to his breathing, sleeping body, mocking her with resolutions unspoken, while outside in the street there are already feet and wheels and in the sky aeroplanes roaring like up-close moths.

So it's not that Mia finds herself falling into the void, ever-widening along the crack in the ice. *Falling* implies the reassurance of landing – which either ends everything or marks a new beginning. It is the reverse of falling: extreme suspension. In darkness, too. Above, there is night. Below, the silence of black water, syrupy, as before freezing. There are no points of orientation at this moment. And no means of wresting herself free by taking a hold of anything that does not slip away even as she clutches at it, struggling. This is the point before drowning, when her senses are erased of memory so that she can see everything with absolute clarity.

Mia knows that getting into this state is what Sam aims at in his work. He said so once. He smiled when he told her, proud of his achievement as well he might be, because he has a degree of control over it. 'That's what happens when I write,' he said happily. 'It's a way of arresting time in the trick of a story. Illuminating a particular instant. Do you see?' 'Sure,' Mia replied to him, 'I see that.' 'You do?' he asked, clearly thinking *like hell she does. She has no idea what I mean.*

'But the thing is, darling,' she had wanted to tell him as she pressed a little harder around his delicate throat, wanting to see her fingers' hard pressure against his jugular so that she could imagine it less easily, 'You're doing for play what happens to me for real.' Put like that, clearly and to the point, it made her feel almost free from it and unaffected by it, safe from harm. But she is not. She lacks the control.

Mia has her eyes shut, closing out the sight of the cracked lake above her. But still she is terrorised by the sensation of suspension in emptiness, where to be without binding connections to anything whatsoever means that she is unprotected, battered and bruised, the whole world become threatening. Trapped, inhuman, between heaven and hell, she is cast into limbo – and who can describe that? There is no way to describe the inscrutable, seamless horror of these moments. At this point, language cannot save her because there seems to be no end to it and no memory of a beginning either. And how can language exist unless stretched out across a length of time? It's a lie, she says to herself, his imagining he can arrest time by writing that it is so. In the beginning, there were no words.

And the worst thing is: once she's through, as now she is, she can't even get a glimpse of how she was then. She opens her eyes, looks up at the crack cutting through the ceiling of her vision. The tiny pale breaks look somewhat like a palm's life-line. Unthreatening. Unengaging. Merely as they appear to be and no more.

But she does not forget. And sometimes, when it is dark, she is reminded of that nameless thing which lurks, soon, always too quickly upon her, an unending-seeming suspension which in fact does end, *has* ended, at least this time, which is the cruellest part of all, because then she feels betrayed.

It is *all she knows*, ripped out from under her. And it tells her that she can be certain of nothing, not even of that pain, repetitive horror that torments her. She is left reeling, bent double and shocked to the limits of her skin. Were she to taste her flesh then, she suspects it would no longer be sweetly bloody but would taste bitter, like one of those odd animals that changes colour when it is afraid. At those moments, she despises herself with such force she has to hide her hands, afraid of what they will do to her.

Soon it will be morning, another day entirely. Mia's face is shivering with the cooling wetness of having cried for hours. *Did I cry for hours?* she asks herself, uninterested. *It's no good crying for the unborn is it? I am not the I I once was, and that only a few minutes, hours ago, so what could I ever have been?* She should be happy to be freed from who she was, Mia tells herself. Some people would pay good narcotic cash to lose themselves so completely, abandoning all recollections of corporeality – all those things that, once verbalised, may make a person suspect the hand of loveliness. But that suspicion is only a fault of language, giving people ideas of certainty beyond their station *and that's the sorry truth it all comes down to* she realises, suddenly no more than despondent, wishing that to be convinced of something could amount to more than merely a loop of words floating along like a dead constellation.

So it all comes back to his beloved words in the end, Mia thinks, feeling the trap snap tighter on her heart. A few shapely marks upon a page – no more than an arid coda to the fear of failure. But certainly, those pretty black scratches on a piece of paper mean less than Mia's kiss, gently, alongside that other woman's immaculate evidence, brazen on his shoulder. And certainly words can't tangle with this deceptive length of days, months, all the lies which he nests about her, cocooning her in deceit. Living as though she trusts him, she exists only in his mad parallel world, a signifier of another's jealousy and fascination, made real through writing. Which is why she wants to wake Sam now from his isolating slumber and make him fuck her, because that would surely mean something. And of course he would concede that much, the inarticulate lure of beastishness really very strong in his heart after all, *that much is true*, she thinks, *I know, you don't have to say anything*.

VI

It is not long before Sam asks Mia to marry him. Turning to her one day, he says with a nervous grin, 'Marry me.' And the inappropriateness of his request, offered as it is with such determination, makes her laugh, saying 'Yes, all right, yes,' as he tumbles her over backwards on the bed, pinning her down laughingly with the sunlight streaming in through the windows – by now it is summer.

'You mean it?' he says, 'You really mean it?' before undressing her, each piece of clothing removed in deadly slow silence as he suddenly becomes quite different to how he was before, almost enraptured. He stares hard at every inch of her body as he reveals it, as though he has never seen it before but at least knows one thing about it: he must take great care. And she knows that for these moments he is in thrall to the notion: *now I've changed everything, just by asking her to do that*. He might as well be shouting this, it is written so clearly across his face. She suspects he is surprising even himself with how excited such intimations of power can make him feel, thrilled to his guts like a child smelling adulthood one springtime.

But Mia feels the rhythm of his body inside her like the rhythm of death: coffin nails knocked into soft wood, the subtle persistence of defeat. They could have been so much more than this diminishing equation of *husband and wife*. Yet he revels in the power of the alchemist, transforming his base lies into the golden fact of marriage. Trusting him enough to say 'yes', she is his apprentice, complicit in his fictions. *But it isn't his fault*, she tells herself, it's really their joint inability to trust in anything beyond the slack net of language, binding them more loosely than ever now, if even at all.

Sam holds her down beneath him, kissing her. She can see the comfort he finds in the joint retreat they are beating, hiding themselves behind the screen of words like wilful children who take great pleasure in tiny lies, learning cynicism faster than walking. *But I wish this weren't true, and especially not of him*, she thinks, looking now along the ridge of his broad back as his muscles bend and crush to fit her, fixing her to the bed beneath him as he mutters heartfelt promises against her ears. She wishes that even one of his promises was still able to affect them, hearing the words *love* and *marriage* floating off into the air above their sweating flesh, utterly ineffectual, just the empty, dried out carcass of a once-felt idea of union now become no more than the word itself.

It is dark. The *husbandwifemarriage* words tighten around Mia's ankles, dead weights pulling her under. She barely struggles. There would be no point. They are stronger than she yet knows how to be. They caress her like reflected lightning, black brilliance before thunder. And sweetly, staringly, she drowns in the limpid chill of a future without herself. When at last he raises his head from her neck, he is laughing with obvious contentment, for which she can't forgive him.

'You really will do it?' he asks, sure that she will. So Mia smiles, at that moment despising him, wondering if she can really be so foolish as not even to go looking for herself beneath this idiot intention of his. 'Yes,' she tells him, turning away.

His face is smiling a wide smile above her when she opens her eyes. He kisses her on the forehead like a guilty uncle before heaving himself off her, rolling over on to the bed to lie beside her. A temporary corpse. Lying here like this she feels herself caught in the slipstream of years rushing around her, the weight of waves pinning her to the ocean's floor as she lies face upwards on the sand, watching the distant rumble overhead.

To think *he has no idea* would be unfair. He has every idea what will happen to them. She can see from his wild, sorrowful smiling that he knows precisely what he is asking of her by this proposal and how great a price they will pay for it. What he doesn't yet realise is that his hope of this ending something between them will end in failure. Marriage will change nothing. But she knows that it is his last chance. He wants to get to the end of this particular story which, for him, is already beyond his control. To call her *wife* will help him to do this. Then he can close the book on this part of his life and move on to somewhere else, liberated for a time from the hands he is afraid he will start to hate. He thinks they would cling to him, were he to try to leave. He has no idea how happy his leaving would make her, eventually.

A few days before, he asked, 'Would you mind reading this?' handing her part of a book he was working on, not meeting her eyes as he almost ran from the house. Thinly disguised, it was the story of their life together. Everything that she suspected and he had denied was in there. His promiscuity. All the elaborations of deceit that made his affairs possible. What is more, her shadowy fears, given to him once in petrified confidence, were now used with medical precision to define a troubled mind.

Seeing this evidence of Sam's unflinching attention, Mia could tell how grateful he felt towards her and she was touched: she hadn't expected gratitude. But she was insulted by his ashamed attempts to brutalise her, to writhe away from what he thought she would do to him. It underestimated her love, which had a strength beyond reason. And certainly, she had never wanted to trap him. She hated to see the edginess rising up in his eyes when he came home later that day, bristling with denials – 'Of course I'm not seeing anyone else! You're paranoid! Crazy!' – as so often he does when he gets afraid of being *tied down, caught, curtailed, not free, possessed, owned, hemmed in* or any of the other words he uses against her in anger, not even seeing how much they describe how she herself feels.

'What! You think I could fuck someone else, walk back in here to you, like this, and then write a book about it?' he had raged on another occasion, returning home with late lips bruised, pupils dilated from recent pleasure. 'How could anyone do such a thing! I love you, remember. Look: here I am. Isn't that proof enough?'

So impeccably did Sam deny this fact about their life together – that he fucked other women – that soon Mia found herself living a shadow-life, with all that was good in it seen through the watery eye of mistrust: doubting his honesty, she doubted all tangible facts and was certain of instants of sensation, merely.

On the day he asked her to marry him they drank with intent devotion, almost fanatically. They didn't look one another in the eye but laughed and sang themselves into the night like wrecked ships sung to the bottom of the ocean by mermaid voices, deceptively soft on the delicate air.

The next morning, lying beside him, she watches the thought of her birth dissolve. She barely mourns its passing. It was such a slight thing, after all. Not even worth the tears billowing out behind her as she sails into this new life with him, almost unable to conceive of the thing that has been lost. She might as well dream of any number of possible worlds, however fantastical, as dream about what she might have been, or even *that she might have been*, so diminished is she by his conjurer's words.

But there's an advantage to this she tells herself, loving the way the cool pads of his fingertips trip lightly along the damp skin of her thighs which feel like the slippery bodies of strange sea creatures. *There's an advantage to being invisible. Some kind of freedom otherwise unattainable* is what she tells herself, feeling the thrill of secrecy dance in her eyes when he turns to her, asking, 'Why are you smiling? Are you happy?' Not in fact a question at all. He never listens to any answers she might give to his questions. And she can tell that he once drew the conclusion: *now I know her.*

Mia wonders at what point Sam thought that he knew her. She suspects that her agreeing to marry him was the final confirmation he needed to fix her, bait-like, on the hook of his scrutinising mind's eye. Fix her and be free of her. Then get down to the serious business of transforming her into someone else. Any number of different women to stride and stagger through his stories: all of them, and none of them, really her, but resembling her just enough to make her guts leap with recognition. Mia inhabits the clothy carapace of his fictional women: he sees who she might have been, had she the strength to break away from him, sure that she doesn't have anything like enough to do that, knowing that her love binds her to him like an unwilling parasite, struggling with need.

Sometimes, he becomes so caught up in his vision of another woman, that Mia can see her in his eyes as he gropes feverishly at her own flesh, crab-fingered and keen, excited at the way she transforms into someone else in front of his eyes. A great magic trick, to be so various and evasive.

Yet it is the dense clarity that comes of being flattened into fiction's two dimensions that hurts Mia the most. It burns cold as ice against her eyes. It is almost impossible then to stop herself falling from the window into the street below for no reason other than to find a way to exist apart from him. *Dying*, in her opinion, being the best way to reassure oneself of this fact.

Now his fingers' soft pressure is against the side of her face. From beyond the open window, the only sound is of dusty trees shivering in the weak breeze from off the river, the hum of occasional cars, phrases of birdsong and nothing more than that, unless you listen harder and chance to catch the sound of creaking buildings about to fall and the deaf shout of undead regret burning through the long blind tide of days. The trick is to be sure to stop before you hear and see anything beyond the very first skin of things.

To be able to stop all further excavation beyond these moments would be a great gift, Mia thinks to herself, Sam's cool hands still softly about her, her eyes shutting out everything beyond their bodies, entwined, and the slow flap of white curtains across the window, the pale play of light across the ceiling, all the time trying not to think of anything beyond the feeling of warm sun on skin and his huge hands' thoughtful caress. And if they could arrest time at this simple moment of being with each other, without their thoughts edging into that place beyond pleasure, then they'd have found a way to be lucky in life.

But who can do such a thing. *It's not even possible* Mia tells herself, watching Sam's back disappear into the next room, soon the thump of books and scratch of a pen as he sets to work, ripping through the pages in fast succession. There's always the giddy tip beyond the brink of such ecstatic instants, the ceaseless fall into whatever lies beyond without even the chance of erasing what went before, which would be something, at least, but never even that. There's always the memory of pleasure to torment her, hanging heavily around her neck as a reminder of the fact that it is now finished, before drowning her finally like a fish returned too late to a river, its flapping gills gulping death, defeated by the sweetness of water. Not even, for her, the constant eye. Only these isolated stabs of life shooting through her like dazzling fire. And in the cool times between flames? Worse than the pain of drowning. Nothing.

VII

Even Mia is surprised at how suddenly it happens: the demand for silence. She hadn't expected that.

It is towards the end of their third summer together. The rotting sun ever-lower in the sky, the parched earth, skittish trees disturbed by an inconstant wind are all making her anxious. *Soon there will be storms* she thinks to herself, watching from the window seat at the top of the house. But the days drag on with no change. He becomes restless. She knows he is still seeing other women. In almost three years of marriage, she suspects Sam has never given up on his nocturnal conquests – though she often wonders what he thinks they might result in. By now, his infidelity has become so much a part of their life together that she can't see the excitement he might find in it. She can only think that, for him, women are like train tickets felt through the back pocket of an old pair of trousers: they give him the comfortable reassurance of escape. But she can see how much it torments him – the fact that he always returns to her.

Sam has never wanted to leave her, that much is certain. Nor can Mia leave him, although she fantasises about it endlessly. She knows he has started to despise himself for loving her; he sees it as a great weakness. She also knows that he values his indestructibility above all else. He has no intention of sinking into the watery darkness with her. But he badly wants to see what goes on there. His curiosity rules him like physical hunger. He feels helpless with it and impotent, too, because of the neediness it entails – for him, the worst form of humiliation there is.

This is how things will end for us Mia reminds herself. *He will merely bale out at the last minute, leaving me alone.* He has never had any intention of following her all the way down. For him, the agony of a story ends with the final chapter. From the very first page, he is safe in the certainty of that ending: everything that follows is merely a dispassionate unravelling of events already concluded. A way of tidying up after the deed is done. Even seeing her drown in her love for him is merely Sam's instinctive way of being attentive, a grim-reaping of material for his next story. He has always been driven by an insatiable hunger for the blood of others. *And he has thrived on mine* Mia admits to herself, feeling the anaemic grip of pity for him. All that is left now is to see how he will escape, because she knows he must. He hasn't the nerve to go any further. Neither the nerve nor the cruelty. A helpless combination. Already, she sees him flagging.

She remembers all the occasions she has caught him off guard, his eyes suddenly heavy with desire as he notices the way she handles a knife. She can see plainly then that he is waiting, almost willing her either to lunge at him with it, or turn it on herself. And then the quick fondness in his eyes when he sees her taking sleeping pills or pain-killers. 'Keep going,' his eyes goad her, richly provocative darts of eagerness as she pops one, two – oh please, more! – pills into her mouth, turning her back on him then, because how can she bear it? His look of longing sickens her.

There was even a time, early one afternoon, when he returned home, unexpectedly, to find her white-knuckled with shame, hitching a doubled-up cord of rope to a beam in the cellar. What had been her excuse? It did not matter. He had described the entire event soon after in a story, although *his* woman had reached a further stage: the husband scooped her up with only seconds to spare before self-strangulation. It was a poetically pictured scene, the intimacy of it precisely rendered from the flesh of facts.

Soon enough, there are telephone conversations. Backroom chats to discuss her. He makes suggestions. Bitter things she will have to do *for her own good*. He does not use the word 'safety' but it is what he means – both her safety and his own. She can see that he has convinced himself that she will kill him, or herself. And as the days of his belief tick by, she starts to believe him, too. Maybe she is beyond help, she wonders, losing her mind in a way that is unfixable? She supposes that must be the appropriate expression for it. Just losing her mind in the hum-drum familiar way that blackens half the world with fear. The closeness of madness has always had the power to make her jump, that much is certainly true.

But Mia doesn't want Sam worrying so much. She pities him for it. More than that, it is so dishonest. All he is asking is, 'How can I escape?' But he thinks it makes him special. He imagines his fear of being trapped implies that his spirit is free: it does not. He has always been an anxious man, someone who dreads change, in spite of his eager 'I need my freedom' confessions. So she listens harder and it is only a short time before she realises what he will do.

It is the first week of October. Summer is still blazing. The only signs of it ending are the wild edges of the wind starting to shuffle through dust-whipped streets, the cooling nights and ever-sinking sun. But still, the earth appears to creak with the expansive effects of heat, and people everywhere are tanned and smiling. They speak in loud voices, tormenting one another with bare flesh, inspiring guilty appetites. The house is becoming oppressive with the long, stale bake of days and Mia finds herself jumping in her sleep at night, sweating with the thought that noises mean something. She craves autumn, is desperate for rain.

'Let's go out,' Sam says to her now as he heads for the door, not looking back to see if she will follow. He has been upstairs for hours, packing her things. They have discussed what will happen. At least, he has told her what will happen. She is to go away for a while *to get better*. It is such a simple solution. The perfect way of erasing the problem: remove her to another place entirely, somewhere out of sight.

He really does fear for his life, Mia thinks to herself, watching him. She can see this clearly when he turns back to her. 'Come on,' he says softly, so light that she can barely hear the words. 'Let's go out and walk. We can go to the heath. It's wonderfully windy – there'll be kites.' Not the words, but the look on his face tells her just how afraid he is. But she can help him to overcome it. Her own life is already done, the ending of it fixed securely in his mind's eye, and so how can she fear for the dark weight of it, when already this: lungs drinking in air strangely, tangled weeds dragging her under, legs kicking the surface of the water for the last time, a purely reflexive struggle.

So 'Sure,' she says, 'let's go out,' unresisting, as he wraps her in one of his old coats, too heavy for the heat but clearly he thinks she needs this protection against the world. Sam takes her arm, too, looping his own through it and she winces with remembering. They walk. It is an afternoon much like any other, but for that one thing: by tonight she will have gone.

When they reach the heath, the wind is arching the treetops and cracking the pale, parched grass in thick gusts as jumping kites crash through the blue above them. They pass the place where once they spent an afternoon together in the oaky shade, listening to the crickets hop on the hillside as the sun burnt past overhead, singeing the meadowgrass beyond the rim of the dusty shadows where they lay. Now she averts her eyes from it. He sees her do this. She wants to say *Stop, enough, is this really the only way?* But she says no such thing. Mia knows that Sam would tire of looking for other ways, eventually.

So she trudges the tilting heath alongside him, turning her face upwards to watch the clouds, liking the clutching pressure of his arm's weight around her. *He's right*, she says to herself. *I need to go away to get better. I dream only of ropes and knives, cadaverous exits into thin air, away from this entrapment. My faint-hearted mind is to blame for this. It lacks the imagination to see beyond itself.* But already the fast-rising laughter grips her, making her shake with its wild strength as it tells her otherwise: these violent voices and brute sensations must add up to something. Indeed, Mia knows that they do. *I haven't imagined everything*, she says to herself, feigning reassurance. Sam flinches when she laughs, swerving his eyes away as though from a scene of disaster. Above them, the crashing birds funnel upwards in brisk, mysterious eddies, ever skywards, and far below, in the curve of the land, the black lake waits horribly behind the willow trees, tempting her.

He has a tight grip on her arm. *He will not let go* she thinks, wanting to wriggle free in a way more than physical, though loving his body's vice like an animal's jaw, clamped to the bone blindly. *But when he's sent me away, how will he hold on to me then?* And still in her line of sight is the trembling lake, blackened by deep clouds overhead, fast-flooding through the paling blue.

He pulls her tighter against him, not smiling as they walk beneath the trees which should be beautiful. Only, their tangling branches threaten her like the weeds' endless drag against her ankle-bones, foul and unseen but none the less felt, which is far worse, the hidden touches darkly sinuous. Sam turns slightly then and points skywards where there are kites, bright-coloured and clustering. Doing this, he loosens his grip on her hand so that she can edge away, out of reach, fast down the hillside before he can catch her, though he does run.

The veins are tightening in his neck. He blocks out the bright sky, towering over her as he rushes just a couple of leaps behind. She can hear the rasping, dog-breathing of his throat's constriction even though she doesn't turn to see, because far below, though nearer now, the beautiful lake, pleasant serenity of darkness, is shivering beneath her, the surface like flame-blackened skin rucked up with pain, though with smooth-shining stretches, too, like silver boiled to steaming point, the soft hiss of the surface as though thin rain is falling.

Now, as she runs, the legs whirling beneath her have a speed not their own but belonging to the surface of the hillside, sped into motion by earthquake urgency. The long, parched grass clutches at her bare legs, whipping her ankles raw, bleeding, with stones flying and hands nearby pointing, faces laughing and smiling. And it is something terrible with these legs flying beneath and behind her like mad earth-animals she has no name for – which is a blessing, at last to have outstripped the word for these flailing things, pulling her downwards to the beautiful lake, dense with reflections, the clouds in it tearing past, even the sky become last-judgment vulnerable, liable to explosions and bright evaporations.

Midway above the whirling legs, suddenly, she is poised as though carved from glass, a delicate leap transfixed like a gnat against the blue, seen in a blink, reddened by the bloodshot lid of a half-closed eye. It is at this moment, when she is etched into a bright, unreachable tableau that she sees his face most clearly. He is like a beady-eyed tiger, watchful of its jumping food, not wanting to let it go until the thing is ragged, made useless with taunting. So the leaping arc ends with his arms looped hard about her, his shouts yelling 'No!' as she is brought to a stop beside the lake, things seeming to crash inside her ears as she stands dead still now like a tree.

The life is almost shaken out of her by his tussling, lifting her off her feet, so that she is unhinged from the world, momentarily, the once-boiling hillside now quiet with smooth, pale, airless stalks of grass, unruffled by the dead wind.

Sam keeps his arms about her and she is glad of that. She makes sure her eyes are shut. She knows that if she looks once more at the lake's wet invitation that his arms will have to break apart to let her slide down beneath the lovely surface where he can't get to her, can't see her, either. No more the fang's suck against her too-thin skin.

By the time Mia opens her eyes again, soothed by the rhythmic rock of flesh to flesh, the lake is merely a lake and it makes her smile. *It looks rather ordinary*, Mia thinks to herself. She can't even see what tempted her about it. It offers neither enticement nor threat. It looks cold. She is certain that the water is deep. There will be mud along the bottom, filled up with duckshit and sinking weeds. The water looks greenish, unenchanted, no more than itself.

She feels guilty and ridiculous. He leads her back up the hillside. She is exhausted with running. Her bones ache as though she has just thrown herself off an imagined cliff, thumping her relieved head to the earth with an idiot crack, finding the ground too soon. Saved as she has been, against her will, she is mocked by gratitude and soothed with ashamed hatred. She wanted to die. She has not yet. It makes no difference. *There is plenty of time for all that*, she tells herself, laughing her head off until her ears ache with the menacing sound of it and she shuts her mouth, detesting the noises coming out of it more spontaneous than puke. She bites her lips together to keep them shut and when he holds his warm mouth against her forehead she bites still tighter to stop her jaw gaping wide enough to fit his flesh *snap snap* between her razor-sharp teeth.

The sun has disappeared. The hillside is cooling. It is late. Along the approaching rim of the heath a black dog trots like a riderless horse, stupid with habit. They bend to the meadow, leaning tight together and upwards, watching their feet's tandem swing. 'We should go back,' he says, staring at the crushed meadowgrass. 'Time is getting on.' What Sam means to say is that they will soon be coming to collect her. But he says no such thing. 'Of course,' Mia says to him, looking at her watch. 'It's later than I thought.' By now they have reached the top of the hill, so they stop for a moment, looking down over the lake and out across the city.

If anyone saw us now Mia thinks to herself *they would imagine us to be a couple like any other*. And they could almost be right, were it not for that differentiating fact of her going away, which sticks in her guts like dead rats, stinking, so that she can't forget it.

Sam leads Mia along the brink of the hillside as though she were blind, guiding her with touches which are soft against the small of her back, but firm. She knows he won't make the same mistake twice. It is over now. This is it. Only a matter of hours, that's all she has left. The wind against her face smells of water and bitter car fumes. She half thinks that mingling with it is the smell of him, his skin and breath, but she is probably mistaken: his face is turned slightly from her. Anyway, she gulps the whole lot down, wondering when she will next inhale this particular combination, thinking *probably never*, so breathing harder as though to scour her lungs out with this smell, fill up the flesh with it so that she can taste it later and remember him, these moments, the whole scene.

They begin the downward slide towards home. She takes a final look out over the city. It suddenly appears unbearably fragile in the thinning light of late afternoon, as though at any moment, trembling, it might dissolve into something of less substance than the wind fluttering up against her face, the branches spidering silently overhead, or the damp sweat's minute drip between their tight-pressed palms.

VIII

Now the house is in darkness. The shadow of the building across the street falls deeply through the ground-floor windows so that inside there is almost no light left. They go into the hallway in silence as though expecting thieves. Their delicate footprints across the marble floor, the softly humming clock, are the only sounds. Sam goes through the rooms, snapping light-switches. Soon the place is flooded with brightness. Too bright. It hurts Mia's eyeballs. She goes to sit beside the window at the back of the house where there is still some sunlight left, although it is so weak that like this, with her eyes shut, she can barely feel it. She suspects that she is merely remembering, not feeling.

She can hear him moving around in the hallway, touching his passport for reassurance, reminding himself how easy it is for him to escape, easier still now that Mia is going away. He has always kept his passport there so that every time he leaves the house he can say to himself, *I may not come back. I'm free. I could go anywhere. Just look. I always have my passport ready, so there's the proof.* She can hear him touching the tiny book right now, and when he comes back into the room his face is serene with guilt and expectation. Secretly, Sam is planning where he will go to when she is gone.

He smiles at her and shuffles in the doorway, transferring his big weight from side to side. *Hurry up! Let's get this over with!* his body says, making her want to weep, yelling *Please, not impatience. Not that. At least don't be impatient for me to go for God's sake.* Instead, in a mild voice, she says, 'Do you think they'll be here soon? Or should we eat first?' He grins back at her, grateful, appreciating the distraction she has offered him: she is perfectly well aware that they will be here for her in half an hour. Six o'clock, that was the time they said.

'Yes, let's eat something. That's a good idea,' he says, too loud, prancing through to the kitchen next door, flicking up the volume on the radio as he fusses in the fridge, turning out a heavy heap of food. Mia can hear him. He starts to whistle.

Beneath her, the chair claws at her thighs, the scratchy straw pricks through the fabric of her coat and dress. Mia presses her hands part of the way beneath her which is more comfortable and keeps them from jumping through the vacant air in front of her face, the compulsive twitch to molest become unbearable. They are better now, trapped beneath her and hidden by her own weight. Her feet, hovering momentarily above the floor, want to stamp in time to the music now tinkling from the radio, and when she wraps them backwards around the legs of the chair, the cool wood heats quickly like a witch-burning, the hot lick up the stake. Her ankles start to sweat.

'Here!' Sam exclaims, bringing two plates through into the room. 'Let's eat!' He puts the food down on the table and pulls out a chair, sits down, Cheshire cat grinning, and suddenly she longs to lunge for him with the knife now glinting wonderfully in the last silver rays of sunlight, dappled with tree shade from the garden. It rests on the plate in front of him. A delicate slip of silver. (One of the reasons she does not slice him from ear to ear is that then he'd never see what such a thing would mean, what it would entail for his life. He would learn nothing. There would be no point.)

Sam catches sight of her eyes watching the knife and stares down at it as though waiting for the thing to leap up at him by itself. He twitches, just once, his nose nervously jumping. *Rabbit*, Mia thinks to herself, laughing. She sits down across the table from him and smiles. He smiles back, starting to eat, talking about something or other, the odd words thinned out in the air between them like a door-jamb draught, indistinct and tremulous. She hasn't a clue what he is talking about, although the words no doubt make perfect sense.

The daylight is almost entirely gone. Mia looks at the window. From here she can see the trees shaking. It is still windy. The shadows rushing through the leaves suggest rain and she wonders *how soon?*

Sam stands up and turns the lamp on in the corner of the room. 'Getting dark,' he says, or some such indisputable fact and she wonders how they reached this point, at what moment they agreed to behave like this towards one another. She forgets. It doesn't matter. 'Let's leave this,' he says, waving at the table, closing his mouth fast to the 'for later' words he was about to use. He goes over to Mia and stands behind her chair, reaching his arms down towards her, holding on tight as though she might slip away from him at any second, just slide down under the table and slither away like a slippery fish.

I don't want to go anywhere just yet, Mia thinks to herself, scared by how easy it is for her to formulate at least that certain thought, a definite desire she can put clearly into words and take a better look at. Sam keeps holding on tight and she hears him repeating her name as if to feed it out through time ahead of them, catching more of the moment than they in fact have left. He reaches down further towards her, gathering her up in his arms which she clings to, turning round, standing up so that they can feel almost the entire length of their bodies pressed together. *I believe nothing more about us than this*, Mia realises, holding him tighter, making him sigh as the air eddies out of him and he sways slightly, shuddering with the impulse of a storm-gnawed tree. But he does not let go and even when he moves her over towards the rug beside the unlit fireplace, breathing heavily like a trampling cow, tired with pacing the leaning meadow, even then he holds on tight.

They sink together to the floor, paired divers clutching wildly to mistaken rocks – direction, weight, all confused – the air bubbles are beautiful though, and hands clinging must mean something, surely, even in drowning. So there they are, going down shipshape together, loyal captains meeting miles under the surface of the sea, half dreaming. Their familiar limbs wind together, tired with struggle, but still, struggling for proximity and feeling themselves to be somehow more clearly themselves that way, made light with abandon.

But like a creature contemplating hibernation, Mia is mapping out each millimetre of his flesh so that later, when she will be hungry, she can look for him and taste what parts of him she chooses. She is being careful, you see, and that matters more than anything else at this moment. She must be meticulous. Attentive to everything. She wants to lose nothing, if she can help it. There is plenty of time for that, *soon* time too and lots of it, rolling out of sight ahead, not even anticipated because still so strange.

'I can't let you go,' he is muttering. At least, Mia thinks those are the words he presses up against her ears, although it could just as easily be 'don't want to let you go,' or perhaps more truthfully 'must let you go.' She doesn't know which it is and suspects it will be a while before he knows himself which one he wants it to be.

From some miles away across town, Mia hears the roar of an engine leaping into life, the car coming to collect her. But she does not try to escape from him, nor cling to him, either. She suddenly feels as nimble as air and watchful. Not weighed down by their clutching embrace, but somehow become the embrace itself: little more than the visualisation of an idea, soon to be a remembered thought. Watching them acting out their final moves together does not fill Mia with the horror she had anticipated, almost hoped for. Instead, she feels absolutely detached from all emotion beyond the hotly burning love of touch, their bodies the only things in the world that matter. Meat and bones, naked of thought and unburdened of anguish, which will be later.

It is six o'clock and so the doorbell rings, briefly patterning the church bells' chime across the square three streets away. There are two female voices outside the door. Careful voices fitting to an even tempo and volume. Awful voices mimicking sanity, sounding crazy for being so efficient.

They are still lying on the hearthrug. When the bell rings,

Sam freezes, dead silent for a moment before sighing too loudly.

'What would they think, to find us like this?' he asks, not meeting her eye as he frees himself from her and stands up, smoothing down his shirt, brushing away imaginary dust.

Mia lies down flat and corpselike as Sam leaves the room. She hears him jostling in the hallway, jumping around with — anxiety? excitement? She has no idea which, although she thinks she hears him pluck his passport from its perch and slide it into his back pocket. He answers the door and, from carpet level, she hears him showing the two women into the room at the front of the house. They are talking as if at a funeral. She laughs out loud, hearing them sound like this, but clamps her hands across her mouth pretty quick, not wanting them to hear her gurgling away like a lunatic, which thought makes her laugh still harder. From next door there is a sudden break in conversation and she imagines the three of them exchanging a *poor thing* look amongst themselves. *This is all for the best* their eyes say to one another, flickering nervously around the room for signs of danger.

Mia lies there for a moment longer. Then she goes across to the window where there is a chair and her coat. She puts the coat on. It weighs a tonne. There are gloves in the pocket and so she puts these on too, but they make her fingers sweat straight away, so she pinches them off again one finger at a time, flaps them around a bit to get the air flowing through them and then puts them back on again. Mia's hands appall her. They always have, *but never so much as right now* she admits to herself with a scowl, feeling like a hangman or secret strangler.

She sits down fast when she hears them making the noises that mean they are coming into the room. So when they do, Mia is ready for them, sitting beside the window with a charming smile plastered across her face. Although she doesn't know quite why her smiling should make them all start back as though bitten. But this is precisely what they do, all at once, in perfect sync, like a stage act, the moment they clamp eyes on her, which makes her laugh, not much more than a little snicker to herself, averting her eyes so they cannot see the way they shine dangerously. *I expect they are shining dangerously*, Mia thinks, or maybe it's just through lack of sleep, and boredom at the stupid inevitability of their white-coated decorum that makes her want to weep, it is so lovely to look at.

'Really perfect,' she says, looking up at them as they advance towards her, strait-jacket at the ready. That is a lie, they have no such thing. But they do advance towards her, smirking and starting to perspire. *Does she bite?* they are wondering, the blatant thought blanketed around them like mothballed cloth, stinking usefully.

'Darling,' Sam says, waggling his hands towards the two people he has with him. 'They're here.'

'Well, hello,' Mia says, smiling like a dutiful dog. They look anxious, so she keeps smiling to set their minds at rest. *There is nothing to fear from me*, Mia wants to say but suspects this would only alarm them. So she keeps quiet, biting her tongue to keep it still and harmless between her teeth while the three of them yak on about something or other, waving their arms around weirdly like children describing things they don't know the names for. Mia wishes they would stop it. She can hardly bear to look, so instead she glances out of the window, watching the ruffling treetops shadowing green as, finally, it starts to rain.

A calm almost like happiness overwhelms her. She feels magnanimous, too, and concerned about the fear which leaps into his eyes when they take her arm – though God only knows why they perform this geriatric gesture.

'Don't worry, darling,' she says, close to Sam's ear, so the idiot crickets can't hear her. 'Don't worry, you're going to be all right,' knowing, even as she says this, that it isn't even slightly true and that he will suffer for his part in this more than she can fathom at this particular stage. Already it makes him cry, tiny hidden tears fountaining discreetly in the corners of his eyes where no one but Mia can spy them. To all the world he probably looks mildly upset and not much more than that. But Mia can see the thundering sorrow begin to drum and rumble around the edges of his poor soft brain.

He will pay for this, she thinks, touching him on the arm like a bird's final swoop for crumbs, knowing that touch has to last her for a long time. She turns away before he sees the look in her eyes, because she knows that that would be far worse for him than the vision already fixed against his retinas. *I don't want to harm him any more*, Mia says to herself, horrified by the things that she appears to make happen around her.

Sam stands on the doorstep, fading behind the curtaining rain as they put her and a suitcase of her things into the car, a clean dark blue car without any scratches on it. *They are careful drivers, no question about it*, she notices, wondering how long the rain will last. Mia sits on the back seat, the fat nurse beside her, pretending not to have her eyes glued to Mia like flies in jam.

But she does, and when Mia slides her a fast, sideways look the nurse turns away with theatrical delicacy, not wanting to scare anyone with her lunatic expression, no doubt.

The car begins to move away down the street. Mia does not turn around to watch or wave at her husband, that dissolving name belonging to someone else and to many others more than to her. She does not turn because there is no need. She sees Sam as clearly as though she were facing backwards. It is as though she is watching him standing there on the doorstep with the rain pounding down around him as he flaps his hand about in the air, wishing he were somewhere else entirely. Then even as he wishes this, he suddenly remembers his back-pocket passport, his little salvation. So now he is thinking *Thank God for that. I'll be all right. How could I not be? I won't let this sorrow trap me. I will escape its clutches as easy as can be. The first plane out of here*, he's saying to himself, already smiling, dreaming of maps and strangers, almost salivating because he is starting to want it all so badly: the fast relief of loneliness he desperately needs.

That is what Mia sees as she is driven away in the wet blue car, hissing through the streets, over the bubbling river spitting raindrops, through the sights and sounds of this place they have lived in together and been happy in from time to time *which is a lovely reminiscence already waiting for me* she remarks to herself.

So now she is not seeing any of the physical facts that flood by her, but a more real, mind's-eye vision of their life together, each scene spooling out behind her, an endless coil of bright events, isolated by memory.

Mia watches this new thing happen with amazement and

curiosity. *I am being unwound* she thinks to herself, slack-jawed as she stands on the sidelines, watching, doing nothing but watch as her life with him unravels behind her, labyrinth-thread succinctly withdrawn, so that soon – she sees it already – there is only pallor up ahead, pale things without sensation or substance.

The rain drums faster on the roof of the car as they curve around a bend in the road. *How soon nothing?* Mia suspects the almost-now and cannot bear it. *There must be something, surely?* But she doubts it, *doubting* become a tiny respite like the hopefulness of waiting – all she has left.

She tries to forget the fluttering tips of his fingers, scattering caresses to the wind, unobserved then, and now already at a lost point in the evaporated past.

Facing forwards, all she sees is this: the stubborn flesh, her own, marching undead onwards. Decaying, but still enduring. The fat nurse's arm, yelping between her teeth, offers her the reassurance of at least feeling something, though. She clings to it as the doctor says 'You must stop! Now!' which makes Mia laugh her head off, it is so fucking accurate, if only they knew.

IX

After leaving Sam, Mia's days ended and began with a closed door, transfixing her in silence, hidden from the world. But this only re-affirmed her sense of insecurity, and she was isolated, absolutely, by the knowledge that every minute of her life was being locked away in a secret room that even she was not allowed to visit.

It started on the day she left, when she saw Sam turn to go back inside the house, the front door swinging closed to conceal him. Every movement forwards, from that moment to this, was curtailed by that same motion: a door, closing. Soon she could feel only the dead room, hidden within her, and no narcotic shock or tricksy sedative could release what lay inside.

Yet mental solitude also meant an excess of freedom, trapping her in the wild glare of an inflamed imagination: without Sam to transcribe her, her brain burned untrammelled, horrifying her with its arcane eruptions which were violent, inexplicable. So she walked along the narrow tunnel of days like a drowsy ghost, transcendent with unwanted secrets which they tried to shake out of her, in vain. For no trauma-blast had silenced her. Her sickness had been spun about her in delicate graduations, sweetened with love.

Days slid into months but no alteration was ever more than seasonal. Darkness and light offered a sense of definition that amounted to a perfect monotony. All around her and hidden inside her, the white room remained the same, and constant, as though watchful. But it has seen nothing, and now, over a year later, nothing has changed: she has waited for him.

'Are you ready yet?' the fat nurse asks her, hands on hips as she slouches, foot-tapping, in the doorway. 'He's downstairs.'

'Yes, yes, yes,' Mia mutters half to herself, 'What's the rush?' So she takes her time, fastening the suitcase extra slowly to infuriate her.

'You have five minutes,' the woman says, leaving the room, stamping away down the shining corridor, her defeated shoulders vulturous and brutal with frustration.

Mia is ready to go, of course. But still, she takes her time, checking over her things carefully, pretending to herself that this is what she is doing when in fact she is just scared, terrified out of her mind with the thought of seeing him again after this long time of separation.

Sam came to check on her once, during the summer, although he didn't tell her he was there. He clearly wanted his visit to be secret, presumably thinking it would upset her. But she knows that it would have upset him far more, to see her determination and clear-headedness. *It didn't take much to cure me*, Mia says to herself, holding up an imaginary bottle of pills. The well-rehearsed lines that mean so little to her.

She goes across to the window to take a final look at the view. *It feels like home* she tells herself, lying. Poplars disguising the perimeter fence, the winding river beyond, hand-picked lawns, all adding up to a dim vision of order that is intended to soothe.

But it antagonises her. The too-bright green, buoyant with vivid light even in winter, is full of menaces and threats.

Mia remembers Sam's visit. She watched him from the window as he paced the lawns, discussing her with the doctor. She supposed that was what he was doing, with his furrowed brow and nervous glances cast up towards her window. She dodged out of sight when he looked up, although once, when he seemed to stare too long, she was sure that he did see her, darting back behind the curtain. Her eyes, darkly pooled in the frame of the window, were latched then, undeniably, with his. He probably thought he imagined it though, or at least that it would be better to pretend that he thought he imagined it. But she could tell that he had noticed her and she pitied his lack of courage.

The fact that he didn't try to see her sickened her heart, blackening it with disappointment. This was months ago. She has almost forgotten it. And she understands why he found it difficult, of course. He was standing in the shade of the wide sycamore tree in the middle of the lawn when he looked up. She felt the twist of memory slip her backwards into a different loop of time, to when she first met him. It was springtime, and his eyes in the street ahead of her invited an easy liaison that soon became something indelible, over-writing everything else.

But this is a different season. Winter is here and there are only a couple of days until Christmas. Sam has come to collect her. Apparently she is well enough to go home, though of course she is no different from when she arrived, emptied of herself as she then was and blank with sorrow, though hating to call it by that name, finding the emptiness too great for words.

And now? A length of erased life with only the vile green outside to taunt her. Mia turns away from the window, suddenly desperate to leave the place.

There is no snow yet but the earth is bright with frost. It is midday. The cold sun weighs heavily in the sky. Insubstantial light makes the land appear too fragile for the marauding figures upon it, which strut and swagger up and down the long driveway. Some of the people here are allowed to go home for Christmas. The scene outside looks like the end of a school term with the cars back and forth, the people jostling around outside, ready to go. There's almost an air of festivity, and she slams the door to her room with a kind of relief that makes her want to jump with it, clenching and unclenching her fists, eager to get away without mishap.

I don't want to come back here, Mia thinks to herself, trying to look calm as she follows the pathway to the outside, the polished plastic clack beneath her feet. She tries not to listen to the babbling voices as she passes people she has spent so long living alongside. For that time, Mia has watched these people, abject with panic, piss, drool and yell like fighting cats, yet still they terrify her. *No, I cannot come back here*, she realises, wondering what will happen next, now she is sure of that much at least, if of nothing else.

As she walks the long white corridor, Mia shuts her eyes briefly, determined not to *spoil things*, or *mess things up*, now that she has been given this chance to get away. She sees the doctor yesterday telling her, 'Don't ruin things for him at Christmas.' And she could have whacked her in the eye for saying such a thing, the nonchalant cruelty of the words. Instead, she smiled.

'Of course not. I understand perfectly,' beaming convincingly from ear to ear. 'It will be good to be with him for Christmas,' she said, pressing her toes to the floor to stop them leaping upwards to dance on the table beside the lolling ink pens. 'We have a house in the countryside, in France,' she carried on. 'Yes dear, I know, he's told me all about it. And you will go there with him by train, that's right isn't it? Do you remember we discussed it before?' 'Oh yes,' Mia says, keeping the smile in place so the doctor doesn't get suspicious. 'How could I have forgotten? We discussed it already. Silly me, forgetting like that.'

But this was yesterday, and today, downstairs, Sam is here, waiting for her. They say that they will *play it by ear*, about whether or not Mia must come back after Christmas. Her own mind is made up. She will not. She tells them no such thing, of course, saying, 'Just as long as it takes to get me better, you know that's all I want.' Secretly, she is thinking: *Better? For fuck's sake! It should be him they're locking up like a rat to experiment on, not me, with the merest bit of chemical nonsense upsetting itself in my brain from time to time. But he, on the other hand . . .*

Mia says none of this. She just makes plans. She knows what she will tell Sam once they are away from here. She realises what he will want to know, *And don't think I won't tell you*, she says to him now, in her mind, watching his face shrink from hearing this, darting from the words he fears will ensnare him. He will offer me the key, goad me to unlock the sealed-room door. And I'll do it for him, too. He'd better watch out. He'll think at first *Tell me everything! The stories I can find here!*

Though soon enough he will be squirming to get away, stopping up his ears with prettiness, making it all charming so that he can sleep at night.

Do I hate him? Do I want to kill him? Mia wonders to herself, feeling her palms start to creep with curiosity.

She looks jaunty and carefree as she swings along the corridor, down the wide staircase and out into the hallway where Sam is waiting, looking downwards as though reading a paper. *But he has nothing in his hands*, she thinks, *so why is his head tipping over that way?* Which is when she realises that he is bored with waiting, and sleepy, too – just as bad. She is wide awake and electric with expectation. At this moment, she can't even imagine sleep.

'Hello,' Mia says to him. 'Are you OK? You look tired.' Sam's head snaps back when he hears her speak. He blinks fully awake, shaking himself upright, looking up in surprise as though not entirely recognising her. He tries to conceal his shock. Clearly, he didn't expect it to be like this. She has no idea what he must have imagined, but not this, that much is certain. It can't be just her once-long hair now cut like a cat's, close to her head like pale fur. It must be more than a haircut, surely? Perhaps it is he who has become unrecognisable, using different eyes?

He recovers quickly. But Mia wants to get out of there, so she looks at the door, 'Shall we go?' Sam stands up, staring hard at her now.

'I rather like this,' he says, clearly surprising himself as he touches her hair, trying to disguise the fact that it is making his eyes water to see her long hair all gone, replaced with this barbaric badge of newness. *Is she the same wife?* He is thinking this so clearly that he might as well have yelled it, taking her by the shoulders to shake out the answer.

They walk through the main door together and out into the moonish winter sunlight. Getting away is Mia's main concern, and Sam almost has to gallop to keep up with her as she slides across the carpark – 'Dodging stray crazies,' she tells him with a wink – towards a car he points out, saying, 'New car.' 'Right,' she says, 'Come on. Let's get going,' almost yelping with relief when they clear the boundary fence and head out into the main road, smooth wheels thundering away beneath them.

'It feels good to get away from there,' she says quietly, trying not to roll her eyes when he says, 'Oh my darling, it's been so long—' Because an expression like that is enough to make her explode at this particular moment. It holds so little sense for her. She has no means of mapping out his 'so long' vision of her absence. How could she even have existed through something so uncharted?

This is not to say that she has forgotten the last fifteen months of her life. *No, that would be insane*, she says to herself, grinning at the view beyond the window. But it is something very like forgetting and far less violent: for the entire length of her time there, Mia stopped. She went unobserved by his writer's eye. Like the unfelt but understood inertia at the high point of a fairground ride, she was silenced by an unreflective horror that was close to death. It was a pause in the flow of her life far more emphatic than waiting.

So as they spin onwards, warm within the incubating car, she can almost hear the creaking heave of time begin to wake up again, the just-heard groan of events still far off but getting nearer. Mia looks out at the flooding trees, the late sun low down against the frozen clouds, the fast houses, and wonders what would have happened to her, had she stayed in that place, with the pale room closed tight around her mind. Perhaps that emptiness would have been *everything*, until one day, unmysteriously, her little heart stopped beating even as her shorn hair and safe-clipped nails kept growing, disgustingly rooted to life.

'But there's so much to talk about,' Sam sighs. 'I don't know where to begin. You look great. I mean, you look really well,' he adds, giggling madly, shooting her a quick look. *Oh well in that case*, she thinks, smiling back at him, touching her hair. 'It didn't seem right, all that hair,' she says, high-pitching her voice to a siren squeak. She can tell that he is relieved, and hungry to know more, already lusting after visions of electric-shock treatments, padded rooms and back-stabbing syringes produced like wicked tricks. He hopes for the worst, can't wait to hear her litany of horrors.

Mia watches Sam closely as he drives. How well she remembers that black light in his eyes. It is there already, even before he has felt his appetite's greasy gnaw take a hold of his guts. His hunger creeps up to him from behind, the jabbing fingers from the crowd, the surreptitious, stolen touches. *It's a curse I wouldn't have for all the world*, Mia thinks, *to be that hungry*. And she wonders what it will take to make him realise that it *is* a curse, not a blessing.

Even now, Sam imagines that his hunger, gratified, is what keeps him alive. She sees the pride creeping into his eyes without him even noticing it, the little plans to *make something of this*. He even imagines that somehow it makes him free, God help the poor misguided vampire *and God help me for ever having fallen in love with him* she says to herself now, feeling sick and suddenly full of fear as she wonders how long will it be before he gets his teeth jammed into her neck, how long before she invites him to do it?

'Hey kiddo, we're going to be OK, you and me,' he says suddenly, his smile dimmed slightly, because of course he doesn't believe this desperate wish for one minute. Sam can tell that she knows this, too, from the fast expression on her face as though she's on the point of running away. It excites him. He loves to chase. *Not yet*, Mia tells herself, looking ahead at the dazzling road, *he can have everything he wants later, but not yet, this is too soon. I need more time*.

'So what we're going to do,' he's saying now, 'is leave the car in town, take the train across to France and then down to the house. We could stop over in Paris if you like? We have one day. Then we can be there in time for Christmas.' He reaches across, squeezing Mia's hand in his. *Only the second touch he has given me so far*, she realises, remembering herself dancing out of his reach when they stood beside the car, thinking *I might dissolve if he touches me, don't touch me yet*, because her hand is already wet with wanting him. She can think of nothing but his touches and how she hates herself for lacking them. She finds it repulsive to be this needy, craving another human being to such a violent degree.

But by the time Sam turns to look at her again, she appears calm, which is a miracle, since her mind is crashing about like a bad machine with fear at having to give him up a second time.

Not now, once is enough. Though she knows that there was never anything so selfless or so simple about it. It was more to do with an intolerable, rock-in-the-eye vision of her life as being reduced by loving him to that one fact and nothing else beyond it. An entire life shrunk into the single act of loving another human being. Just a piece of flesh that loves another piece of flesh, senselessly. And who can tolerate a life so small as that, diminished to one naked need? Who can do such a thing, be forced to admit it, and still stay sane?

He will not have everything just yet, Mia shouts to herself, chastising her sledgehammer brain to keep it quiet while she tries not to dig her nails into the flesh of his hand which still holds her own loosely within it in a way that is no doubt supposed to be reassuring. But it enslaves her, as though it is not her hand but her heart that he holds so casually.

The day is brightening into the start of a perfect midwinter afternoon as they approach the station. *I will give him what he wants*, Mia says to herself, *and more than that*. But first, she needs some time with him that is not spied upon by his writer's eye. Just a few days where they have lived together, as if that was all they had and all he wanted. So that at one point in their lives, there will have been something between them that was sacred and secret. Something that he will not bastardise into a book for other eyes to gloat upon.

He must not write about these days together, Mia says to herself, looking Sam hard in the eye so she can be sure he sees that this is what must happen.

He seems to understand, raising her hand to his lips, kissing each finger in turn, shutting his eyes as he says, 'I'm with you now. We're going to be alright.' Mia scrutinises his face, wishing she could trust him. She suspects that she cannot. And she wonders what she will have to do to rebuke his desperate conviction that all life, however precious, can be converted into more-precious words.

Let him see how wrong he is she says to herself, watching his beautiful mouth turn to her, his lips trembling in anticipation.

X

They take the train to Paris, spend one night there, then on to another train and down through the countryside to the house. What happened then, in the space of just two days, was her final proof. Nothing had changed.

The shadows are lengthening and fading to black, and the long trees are leaning silently beyond the thick glass of the train window as, at last, they arrive at the station.

They get in the car and drive on into the night. Sam describes everything to her just before it happens, picked out of the darkness by the headlights as they pass by. 'Soon there'll be the farm where – remember that massive oak tree? It blew over in the storms last winter, you can see it fallen right through the barn beside the house. Then the village, they shut down the bakery. We have to get bread from town now. I'm sure they'll open another one soon though, everyone was up in arms about it.'

He prattles on in this way until at last they turn off the main road into the driveway, bumping through the long avenue of ash trees to the house. There is a lamp on inside and the yellowing light seeps out across the frosted earth. 'I had forgotten quite how beautiful it is here,' Mia says to him softly as they get out of the car and stand for a moment in the night, speaking in whispers as though afraid to wake someone, although the house stands alone, surrounded by fields and trees on the brow of the hill. The nearest neighbour is on the far side of the valley. Their farm is just visible, standing at the top of the distant ridge like a lighthouse, partly hidden amongst the waving trees, mountainous troughs glistening in the night.

There is almost no sound now, apart from the faint crunch of earth as Sam walks around the car towards her, pulling her tightly up against himself and holding her there so that she feels like a grateful animal, wordless, loving to be held. They stand like this for what seems like a long time, the cold night air pushing them closer together. Soon Mia begins to catch the sound of other things: pine needles from the forest, cracking with frost, the whisper of a faint breeze sliding across the half-frozen lake in the valley below, the pigeons' ruffled feathers as they move around through their sawdust sleep in the barn, and all of this adds up to a calm night with two watchful people beneath stars. That's all it is. A Christmas Eve night like many others already past.

Sam goes up to the house ahead of her, swinging open the door so that she is lit up suddenly, speared against the black night. She cannot see his expression. He is silhouetted against the brightness from inside. But he holds the door open and she reads his gesture as a challenge, provoking a trust that she can ill afford. She walks towards the open door, he guides her inside with a hand that feels like kindness against her shoulder-blades. But the door's sharp snap shut makes her wince and Mia knows that it is too late.

The housekeeper has been in to light a fire in the kitchen and the whole scene appears blissful-calm as things settle into night. He says, 'Glad to be home?' And the words taunt her. She wishes she could take hold of *gladness* and *home* and run somewhere with them bannering out behind her like triumphs. But she cannot loosen the fear that they will never happen to her again.

'Oh I am glad,' Mia tells him, with more hopefulness than honesty. Holding him in her arms more tightly than before, she presses her face against his chest so that she can inhale his skin and shut out everything that is not him.

The night stretches itself out around them. 'Nearly Christmas,' he tells her softly, leading her by the hand upstairs and into the unlit bedroom. 'My darling wife,' he says, clinging to her, his hands edging closer to her neck. 'I'll never let you go again. Help me understand,' he whispers, his shoulders curving around her in a protective embrace that makes her feel unsafe. She knows what he is asking of her. She hears the urgency in his voice even before he realises it is there himself. He won't be satisfied until he has every last drop of her blood and then what? What will she do then? She has seen his back too many times not to know how desperately he longs to escape.

The curtains are pulled back from the windows and high up in the velvet sky there is a full moon sailing through the bright nest of stars so that down below, the little room is awash with incredible light. It turns them into luminous swimmers, many miles under the sea. They undress one another, watching closely. His eyes goad Mia on, saying *Soon, you know it will be soon*, the magnetic pull towards satisfaction, and when she catches sight of his teeth lit up with moonlight she shuts her eyes tightly, not wanting to see their eager mastication.

'Are you cold?' Sam asks, wrapping himself around her more tightly and wriggling down further beneath the blankets. He heats her face up with kisses, hot-breathing tenderness against the side of her neck.

By the time they unfold themselves from one another, Mia can feel the heavy calm of sleep weighing his limbs against her. But she cannot sleep. Sam tips her over towards him, drawing her closer.

'I promise—' he starts to say, until she kisses him to stop the words. 'What?' he asks, smiling. 'I want to keep you here, and safe, I was going to say,' he tells her, stroking her hair with tiny fingertip touches, almost implausible with hands like his, better suited to violence. 'I want you to tell me everything, too – if it helps,' he adds.

'You,' she says, smiling nervously. 'Asking questions.' Mia touches the outline of his lips with the tip of her tongue, watching the quick hope crackle in his tindered eyes. 'Don't worry,' she says. 'I haven't forgotten that I said I'd give you the whole story. You want to know everything?'

Sam takes a tighter hold of her, eager fingers feeling violent with relief – and something else: the effort of controlling his confident satisfaction, which Mia knows is improved with delay. 'Yes, please tell me everything. But now it's late. Tomorrow?' he says. And she can almost feel the blood rise up in his brain in expectation, though she knows it will not stop him from sleeping.

'Yes, tomorrow,' she tells him, turning over so that he does not see the fine hatred of defeat stamping through her eyes.

The moon is obscured by trees and the room is silent, darker than before. He is sleeping, and when Mia eases herself out of bed, careful not to wake him, she can hear his arm slither back through the sheets, wrapping itself around his own body instead of hers. She stands for a moment beside him, watching his vulnerable sleep through darkness.

Her eyes adjust to the gloom. Even without light, she knows that on the table, within arm's reach, there is a slim silver letter-knife, beside it, a heavy lead crystal paperweight, and nearby, a coiled leather belt with a wide buckle, perfect for puncturing a fatal artery – any number of innocent objects that all ideally articulate her murderous intention.

They were right, Mia thinks to herself, *I'm unsafe. He is foolish to slip into sleep with such trusting abandon*. Her hands stroke the surface of the silver knife, cool as contemplation. *He has feared for his life with good reason*, she admits, weighing the blade for pleasure in her palm.

Mia knows that this is the way Sam expects the story to go. He has written such scenes so many times. But her resolve is flagging, and she disbelieves the neatness of the equation: kill him, be free.

The exposed column of his throat is pale against the paler sheets. She touches the skin with the tips of her fingers and presses the fluttering jugular with a kiss. As she raises her head, her teeth catch against her lips. She tastes blood. He does not stir. His face is calm, untroubled. She watches the faint flicker of dreams twitching his eyelids as he sighs slightly, a tiny whistle of sound as she turns away from him and pads silently from the otherwise noiseless room.

Outside the bedroom, in the long corridor running the length of the house, there is no light apart from a faint yellow glow from the lamp left burning in the stairwell. Mia goes downstairs and out of the house into the night.

She stands on the hard earth in her bare feet, pulling Sam's heavy coat more tightly about her as she gulps in the cool air which makes her shiver straightaway it is so icy, almost burning her lungs. From inside the house, she hears a clock's muffled midnight chime and then she sets off across the stiff grass towards the trees. There is no wind and the air is bright with stars. Beyond the furthest edge of the forested land she can see the halo of hidden moon beaming upwards into the sky and she knows that soon it will rise higher, lighting up the land again. Her naked feet feel like cold rocks. They are starting to bleed. Even though she can't see them, she can feel the wet blood's warm ooze on to the stony ground.

Soon the earth starts to tip slightly, curving downwards through the trees and so she walks among them, looking upwards through the branches at the sky. Mia has always been afraid of trees at night. She wishes that she had tried to conquer that fear and wonders if that is what she is doing now. She feels almost proud as she marches on alone through the thickening forest, downhill, towards the lake.

She catches glimpses of the moon, risen above the far side of the valley, a miraculous disc of light that makes her blink with pleasure. She snags her breath on it, feeling the pain of leaving trip up in her throat, tightening.

Mia shuts her eyes for a second. Her brain is burning up, she wishes it wouldn't but she can't stop it – those impotent thoughts in fast succession, smashing into one another as she opens her eyes, watching herself walking out of the forest and into the lame wet grass beside the lake.

The long green blades are billowed into brittle stillness like a transfixed ocean. Motionless, Mia stands there on the edge of the forest, taking in the whole scene, thinking *I don't want to miss a single thing*. Nothing must escape her now. But how she wishes she could see everything at once: the blackening trees, dangerous with starlight, the curve of his lips rushing to meet hers, the cool explosion of noise between blood vessels inside her brain, even now as she stands there dead still, watching.

So next her bleeding feet are wading through the tall grass no longer silent but lisping softly against her toenails. She steps through it, high-stepping like a meticulous gazelle, towards the lake. It is almost a matchless circle like the moon, but half frozen and tipped on to its side as though enduring silent death throes. Mia longs to hear them. So she presses her ear to its delicate surface to hear the thin scream of water as she inhales it deeply, thinking of Sam's skin which smells precisely like this, of cold lake-water pressed tight up against her nostrils.

All things lead to her love, of course, since she is no more than that, nor has she been since she first set eyes on him, that day when there were too many people crushed about her in the street, none of them him, and then there he was. Everything after can be found in the slippery pages of his books. Nowhere else. Not even on his lips which lie when they say things, but never when they shudder slightly as they do when he writes things down. *And isn't the world crammed full of sadnesses such as that one?* Mia thinks to herself as she wades out towards the thin ice which cracks beneath her crashing hands as she breaks it, wanting to get further beneath it to the warm isolation, so at last she can get a glimpse of herself with him not there to see her.

Then the ice is above her head and the bubbles sliding upwards to the night where the moon still shines more watery than before. She can see it through tear-filled eyes stretched wide open like her nostrils, lungs, drinking the whole lake into her if need be and the fishes too – although she expects that like him they are sleeping, nestled tight among the tugging weeds which tangle her ankles, pulling her further to where she wants to be, which is as far as she can get down there beneath the hidden dirt at the bottom of this beautiful lake, murky with solitude as it should be and so it is.

Though now, even when she's in the thick of it, with her eyes wide open, even now, drowning, at last wrestling herself free of this thing, herself, that does nothing but love him without sense beyond flesh, even now as the albatross weight pulls her under, all she can see is his face.

So she shuts her eyes, smiling.

I t is around one o'clock on a winter's morning. Unmoving, the writer has been slumped over his desk for most of the day. His hunched shoulders, bowed head and oddly contorted attitude might make someone mistake him for a dead man, if they chanced to break in upon his silent reverie. But his is the only house for miles and he is entirely alone. He says that he prefers to work like this, in complete isolation, undisturbed.

Beside him, on the desk, lies evidence of his labour, now completed. A few inches of typescript-heavy manuscript, neatly stacked and dense with amendments.

The light on the desk beside him flickers slightly and it is this change, in the otherwise motionless room, that revives him, for he lets out a delicate sigh of exasperation at the subtle reordering of his thoughts. He reaches for another sheet of paper, positions it in the quavering pool of light and writes: *The first and last time Sam saw Mia, her back was turned.*

Then he pauses, his brow wrinkled in a frown as though wondering whether that was, in fact, true. Yet this *is* how he will always remember her – turning the other way. Although in anyone else it might have been frustrating, that exclusion, it offered him what he most needed: secrecy.

With her head turned from him, he could sustain his sense of freedom. She couldn't spy on what he was up to. And he needed this solitude to be able to write. It was the most tenuous sort of freedom, but it worked. He clung to it like a drowning man.

Now she's gone he can be free, absolutely, he writes, finally turning from the window, settling deeper into his chair, pulling the blanket he'd taken from off the bed closer about him, protection against the midwinter chill, the air noiseless apart from the scratch of his pen, the grating rhythm of the clock downstairs.

It was almost as quiet as this the night she left, he remembers, enjoying the secret symmetry of the year's lapse between then and now. But her silent retreat did not surprise him. She had always been horrifyingly elusive. Definable only after the deed and so then already changed by it. Apart from her, he had never encountered anyone who, in the space of a few seconds, could become unrecognisable to him. *Although Sam knew this was partly his fault*, he writes in the margin, *still, he often wondered: was she ever really his?*

Now, sitting here like this, the cold silence of the empty room gripping fast around his throat, he can feel the weight of their time together crushing him just enough to make his hands shake with the pollution of excess memory, humiliating him – a man so unused to being humiliated – cowing him instantly.

The way he told the story, she crept out into the night unnoticed, and while his back was turned.

But in fact he was not asleep. His soft nocturnal purr was a hard-hearted simulation, thrilled with dread. He even saw her leave the room through his fluttering eye-corner, feigning dreams. And with the milky moonlight around him, warm sheets to swathe him in comfort, he had felt his thoughts already germinate into a plan for a new book. He heard the front door's click, too, and when she started to glide across the lawn, sliding like an angel through the night, away from the house towards the forest, the lake, he watched her from behind the curtains, knowing exactly what she would do next, perfectly able to stop her, had he chosen to.

You see, he always knew how the story would end. From the first moment he set eyes on her, he knew how it would finish between them: one of them would have to die. And he knew it must not be him, although he often feared for his life – that much had been true. He noticed the way she had a habit of averting her eyes from sharp objects. She had even admitted one time – he remembers how it horrified him – her unbearable fascination for necks. Now, in his mind's eye, he sees her slip away beneath the moon, her pretty ankles dancing across the wet grass, down through the dark towards the icy lake. He had always been sure it would happen, sooner or later. He had even goaded her to do it, if he's honest with himself, wanting her to give him back some measure of the freedom he had felt before he met her, never since. And he granted her the poetic justice of Christmas Eve, although he still didn't see the sense of it.

The darkness surprised him, though. He knew how much she hated darkness. How deeply she feared being left alone in the pitchy strangeness with nothing but unseen terrors lurking, everything reduced to the pungent murk of spiky touches – he knew this terrified her.

Seeing her enter the edge of the forest made him wince. He

anticipated her fear. Did she falter? Perhaps he imagined it, but he could have sworn he saw her feet trip up slightly, as though reluctant to dive into the dark well of trees and night unaccompanied. But it must have been a trick of the light, because if he tries to picture it again, there, she's already gone, swallowed up by the forest as though she stepped into ink, without a splash or intake of breath, no air bubbles to betray that she had been there at all. He can see her now, her back turned to him as she leaps empty-handed away, not looking round, appearing almost light-hearted – if he didn't know better, remembering the humiliation of that huge coat of his which she is choosing to wear now, of all times, see, she's wearing it now.

Of course, this means that he is admitting, too late, that he saw her strength and the strength of her love for him, if that is the word for it. It mocked his own weakness, depriving him of all autonomy. And truly, he was never in possession of himself at any moment after he met her. Loving her was burdensome to him. He was grateful for her alleviating gift of death: it had given him a great story. He also assumes that this had been her intention, her way of giving him everything. How idiotic it is, he notes with a disgusted scowl, for people to promise to give themselves entirely to one other. Do they even know what that would mean? For sure, *she* had known all about that, he thinks with a pang of admiration, and her suicide had been ample proof of the power of fiction. In the beginning were his words. She had merely followed the trail they set out for her.

Yes, it was certainly a true story, no doubting that, he commends himself as he sets his pen down – apart from their names, changed to avoid the charge of autobiography. Even when it cast him in an unfavourable light, he had kept his steely gaze fixed on the facts, and in this way her epitaph was an honest one, as far as he knew. He imagines her pleasure in seeing the courage it has taken him to do this. Then he reminds himself of her death – that it is real in a way he cannot shuck off – and he is irritated that she will not witness his bravery.

It was a bitter disappointment to him, that she denied him that final glimpse into her heart by leaving him the way she did. And although he had tried, he couldn't write about those long months when she was apart from him before – her secret life shut away from his meticulous gaze. Perhaps he lacked the imagination? he asks himself with a disbelieving smile.

He remembers how he lay awake the night she finally left, half waiting for her to come back, knowing that she would not. Am I waiting for her still? he asks himself with a deep sigh, flexing his fingers at his sides as though to scoop up the words he has lost. What is the expression for waiting when there is no chance of an end to it? A kind of limbo. Not good. Distracting. There must be a word for this. It is something like missing a person, but far more mysterious and weirdly devoid of value, too, because of the absolute hopelessness implicit in it. It is like a sound at the back of his mind that echoes the intricate fathoms of her absence. But without pleasure, and too loud to be merely regret. No, he tells himself, there is no word for this.

But still, he is glad of his unerring truthfulness. It is something entirely new to him. More than that, it has afforded him the levity of a confession. Already, he relishes the unfamiliar liberty that comes of having told the truth (with the exception of the ending – the fatal fact that he could have stopped her leaving as she did; but how could it have been otherwise? He had told it from her point of view, and she had not been aware of his pretence of sleep, those secret theatrics. Or had she?). Whatever the truth of it, he feels hopeful that he has finally cast her off: the alchemy of igniting facts with fiction and watching them burn, becoming harmless.

On finishing, his only remaining anguish is a selfish one: can his confession lift the dead weight of guilt from around his neck? Admitting his part in her death – and freely, too – he also sees his foolishness in thinking he could ever truly forget her, and worries that all his memories of her will, inevitably, be weighted with misgiving. She is lodged heavily inside his heart now, even more emphatically than before. Missing her – if that's the word for it – he won't be able to avoid fantasising about her possible future incarnations. Already, he feels haunted, anticipating her ghost in as yet unwritten books. But he pushes these thoughts aside. Really, they are of no importance. Just words.

He looks out into the deep night, scanning the empty land with restless eyes. But he can still see those feet, disappearing into the icy forest, and soon the still icier lake.

He tells himself that he is glad he has finished writing about her. His sense of it being over was like recovering from a sickness, though he is still aghast at it, even now, the memory of suffering clinging about him and lingering emphatically, as only the scent of sick people can: not unwashed but unclean.

'But it is over now,' he says out loud, hating the sound of his voice, unanswered, in the musty room. He shuts his eyes, but he can still see the darkness close over her slender back. It was a vision that had always bothered him: the completeness of her disappearance. *Now I am alone and I can see myself clearly, without this disturbance of love,* he breathes out in pretence of satisfaction, reminding himself that this is what he has always sought – with every woman cast aside, every book completed. *I need never write about her again,* he says to himself, trying to imagine the relief he might find in that freedom.

Turning back to the empty room, he lays his hand upon the pile of manuscript, lightly caressing the word-spattered skin of the last page. He contemplates the finality of his book's conclusion and tells himself that it is a job well done. Although I suspect that even now, he is troubled by one thing: he would not have chosen it to end this way.